NECESSARY RITES

By the same author

CAVE WITH ECHOES
THE SOMNAMBULISTS
THE GODMOTHER
THE BUTTERCUP CHAIN
THE SINGING HEAD
ANGELS FALLING
THE KINDLING

England Trilogy

A STATE OF PEACE
PRIVATE LIFE
HEAVEN ON EARTH

A LOVING EYE
THE HONEY TREE
SUMMER PEOPLE
SECRET PLACES
THE COUNTRY OF HER DREAMS
MAGIC
THE ITALIAN LESSON
DR GRUBER'S DAUGHTER
THE SADNESS OF WITCHES
LIFE ON THE NILE

For Children

THE BIRTHDAY UNICORN
ALEXANDER IN THE LAND OF MOG
THE INCOMPETENT DRAGON
THE KING AWAKES
THE EMPTY THRONE

NECESSARY RITES

JANICE ELLIOTT

Hodder & Stoughton
LONDON SYDNEY AUCKLAND TORONTO

British Library Cataloguing in Publication Data
Elliott, Janice, 1931–
  Necessary rites.
  I. Title
  823.91 [F]

ISBN 0-340-53625-X

Published by Hodder and Stoughton,
a division of Hodder and Stoughton Ltd,
Mill Road, Dunton Green, Sevenoaks, Kent TN13 2YA
Editorial Office: 47 Bedford Square, London WC1B 3DP

Typeset by Hewer Text Composition Services, Edinburgh
Printed in Great Britain by St Edmundsbury Press, Bury St Edmunds
Suffolk and bound by Robert Hartnoll Ltd, Bodmin, Cornwall

For Alexander Cooper
with love

ONE

T he place. This is meadow-land, a flattish countryside where willows flourish. In winter the rivers flood and water, lying on the fields, freezes, exchanging signals with a low sky. In summer, soft-eyed cows graze knee-deep in buttercups.

From the Franklands' house, a little way out of town, it is impossible to see the industrial estate, the housing estate, the Japanese software factory or the motorway. Simply the canal in the distance, fields, a lane, a few pleasing houses that have settled over the centuries into the land, farms. For anyone seeking a prelapsarian image, this might once have been Eden.

Moira Frankland is sitting at her desk. The light is the white end of blue. Dan designed this house. This is the house that Dan built. Moira remembers the plot empty on a spring day, the relationship between the sky and the trees and the place their house would fill. Above which it now soars. From certain angles its planes, set against the levels of the small hill, appear unsupported. The swimming-pool is empty.

'I'm sorry? You said something?' As Dan comes in Moira looks up.

'But we'll have the party?' he says.

'Why not?'

'I mean your mother.'

'She's ill. No reason not to have the party.'

'Then we will.' Dan's cheek against hers. Moira raises her face. Habit. Love. The years and years between them. Dan says: 'Shall I order the booze?'

'We'll make a list first.'

7

'Oh, yes. Lists. Right. You make a list.' He pulls on his sheepskin coat. Outside the snow is unmarked, a lemon slip of sun behind the conifers. 'You working here today?'

'Might go out. The library. Mother.'

Dan nods. He is looking out of the window.

'Have you noticed a van in the lane? Over there.'

'No. Why?'

'Nothing. I just wondered. Bye.'

He's gone. The crunch of tyres. The snow is spoiled.

Moira's desk is heaped with books and papers. She is a teller of fairy tales. This morning she has been reading Hans Andersen's story of the mother who lost her child and on the way to Death wept out her eyes. She snaps the book shut, looks at the two sprigs of winter jasmine in the green vase.

The house hums behind her: electrical messages in wide, white, vacant rooms. Dragging her hair into a braid, pulling on her son Sam's old anorak, Moira feels that she is the only disorderly thing in this house.

It's so warm in here, yet this could be the Arctic. A frozen world.

The television is talking in the kitchen. As Moira pours herself a mug of coffee and clears the breakfast table, the television tells her that this weather comes straight from Siberia. Normally it stops there. This year it has dashed in from the east to plunge the whole of Europe into an Arctic zone.

So much for the greenhouse effect. The Australian spring has not arrived. In Melbourne floods fifty people have lost their lives.

After his sister Lucy died, we talked about Sam all the time. It was easier than talking about Lucy.

As it turned out, perhaps we were looking for trouble where there was none. Sam seems fine now. When he was eight or nine there was a period when he came home from school twice a week with a bloody nose. He was not afraid. He simply refused to fight back. How do you teach your own child to hurt people?

Dan couldn't help. We talked about it in bed in whispers.

8

To some degree the old stereotypes cannot be shaken off. It is the father's job to instruct his son in violence. Dan rejected his role. He turned over and pretended to be asleep. How could I blame him? (That was the time of the big contract, he was hardly ever home those days, except to sleep. I thought, not very seriously, that he might be having an affair. With his secretary, with any one of the women in the office. With any of the university girls who turn up at parties with bare feet and grubby hair and pale lips and a passion for Dan. He is their centaur. They love his wiry, grizzled locks, his air of a tired lord of misrule, his limp since he tore his Achilles tendon and was months in plaster, raging. They mistake his weariness for wisdom. That is what the toad in my head says when I allow it to speak. On the good days, I am ashamed. It is equally possible that I mistake his wisdom for weariness.)

This blue light is alarming. Especially in the north-facing kitchen. A most efficient room, humming and buzzing and thrumming with ergonomic wizards. Even at night they continue to talk, each magical machine, so that in this open-plan house prowling insomniacs are startled by the high voice of the Italian freezer, the boiler changing cycles.

When they are going away Dan sets the control that turns on the radio all day and the lights after dark. Sometimes the control goes ape and they can hear the radio chattering and singing to itself all alone. When Sam was small they came back to find the baby-sitter in despair. Sam had locked himself in his room. He said there were goblins in the kitchen. In the play area which connects at one level with the kitchen, at another with the living area, Sam at seven or so pitched his wigwam, coming out only to eat or sleep. His failure to grasp the high ideal of open-plan (that everyone should have access to everyone else at all times) disappointed Dan who crouched outside his son's tent and attempted to reason with him.

Moira did not intervene in this exchange. It is all right now, anyway. When Sam is home he lives in his room, decorated to his own taste. That is to say, he spends most of his time lying on the bed, ears plugged into ferocious music,

9

watching the flickering images on the small Japanese portable television. Still blu-tacked to the wall, though out of date by years, are posters for the Stiff Little Fingers and Motorhead. Also a French poster for Dieter Jung's holography, blown-up photographs, black and white, of rather good nude studies, and the first poster Moira remembers him bringing home: *Due to lack of interest tomorrow is cancelled.*

Moira feels strongly that children should have their privacy but every so often she looks into Sam's room to see what is new. The graffiti are becoming increasingly cryptic. Last week it was: *Reason is the pragmatism of incomprehension.*

He has taken the legs off his bed and sleeps on the floor.

There is a very beautiful picture of an androgynous figure wind-surfing.

He has painted the ceiling red.

In the kitchen the wall-telephone rings. Moira snaps off the sound on the television. The images persist. A fire bomb in Belfast. Under martial law tanks have joined the armoured cars. Nervy, exhausted food queues in the snow. The new reporting restrictions mean the hunger riots cannot be shown (unlike those in Eastern Europe). Sweet snow falls on the dozing tank.

'Hello?'

'Moira?'

'Sorry. Kate?'

'Well, of course it is. You said you were going to ring. What are you doing? Are you still there?'

'I'm here.'

Kate. Moira's friend. University wife. Has just been ditched by Howard, Dan's partner in the architectural practice and part-time University lecturer (and lecher). It has become a legendary joke that Howard Summerson got his lectureship on the strength of a prize-winning Brutalist cowshed in Schleswig Holstein. Nowadays he concentrates on what he and Dan call the carriage trade: converting barns and butter-mills for well-heeled commuters.

In Dan's view Moira spends far too much time coping with Kate Summerson. I'm not coping. We're friends. That doesn't stop because she's in trouble. (Oh, virtuous-seeming woman, admit it – I can still laugh with Kate. We had the summer days together. The best.)

'Are you in the kitchen?' Kate sounds tremulous.

'Why?'

'I can always tell when you're in that bloody room.'

'How?'

'Because you sound as if you're going out.'

'I am.'

Moira sits down at the table, the cord just reaches. With one hand she tries to pin up her braid. This weather makes her hair crackle. On the north side of the site only a few conifers have really taken. Even they may not survive. Everything seems to be dying this winter. Still.

'You know the latest? Dan's putting in voice response control.'

'What's that?'

A shower of pins. Wear plait down today.

'You tell things to turn themselves on. You know – light, cooker, boiler. Even furniture. Doors. Shut, door. Oven, cook.'

'My God, sounds like one of your creepy fairy tales. Whose voice?'

'Don't know.' Moira yawns. 'Anyone's. Mine, I suppose. Perhaps it doesn't matter who's talking.'

'Crazy.'

'Yes.'

'If you ever go barking mad, it'll be in that kitchen.'

'Probably.'

'Look. I was thinking, is the road clear?'

'Dan hasn't come back so it must be.'

'Well, we might come over? Poppy and me. She's got a rash so I kept her out of school. Obviously it's psychosomatic. No temperature. Howard was here last night. She didn't see him but when he'd gone I found her on the landing, listening. If he knew the damage he was doing. If we could. I'm much better. I've stopped the crying jags. Moira, are you still there?'

'Yes.'

11

'And this weather. How can anyone function in this weather?'

'I rather like it.'

'What did you say? We'll be there in half an hour then?' Katie says. She does not give up easily.

'Katie, I'm sorry. I really have to go out.'

'I've got chains on the car.'

Coffee's cold. Where are my boots? What for supper? Ought to make thick winter soup. But would need bones. No bones. Potatoes, leeks, carrots, chicken stock cube? Maybe not soup.

'They're skating to work in Amsterdam. Have you seen it?' No one says read any more. There is something sticky in Sam's pocket. Melted Bounty bar.

'How d'you know?'

'It's on the telly.'

'Or you could come to us?'

Moira sighs. 'I'll try.'

'D'you know what happened last night? Howard actually tried to get me into bed. With Poppy listening! And he says I need a shrink. You're so lucky, you and Dan.'

'Kate, I've got to ring off now. Call you later.'

'Oh, Lord. Of course, I forgot to ask – your mother. How is she?'

'Same.'

'You're not having the party this year?'

'Dan seems to want it. I don't see why not.'

'In the snow?'

'It's not snowing indoors. Yet.'

Moira hangs up the telephone. She pictures Kate in her draughty muddly kitchen in the terrace of Victorian houses known as University Row. Something was always happening there or said to be happening. Wife-swopping, husband-swopping, seduction, suicide – oh, the wildest tales of which perhaps two per cent were true. Though one summer there was that boy who burned himself to death. That was true. He ran into the street, a living torch.

For a wonder, the paper has arrived. The world goes on,

tick tock. Snow in Nice. Iceland the hottest spot in Europe. Two hundred dead in France. In Spain a waiter is found frozen to death on his doorstep with the key inserted in the lock. In America another abortion clinic bombed. Packs of wolves roam the mountains of northern Italy.

Does Sam have frightening dreams?

Upstairs, searching for her thick sweater, Moira looks out of the window over fields of snow. She can just see the lane that leads into the main road. Several times in the last few weeks she has noticed a yellow van parked there. What can it be doing? Wrong time of year for lovers.

From the south-facing window the pool, harmlessly empty, a drift of leaves beneath weakly melting frost. They have not yet brought themselves to use it again. She remembers it filled, on a still blue morning, its face bland. Lucy drowned there. Time seems to have frozen over that small body. Moira cannot afford to think about that.

On her way back upstairs to tell Sam she is going out, Moira pauses at her desk, sits down for a moment, half-wishes that someone would tell her: rest, stay.

There is a snowstorm paperweight her mother gave her that she has used for twenty years. Which she now shakes, sitting at her desk, wondering. Shall I go out? Shall I ring the hospital? Shall I write?

The flakes settle on the miniature scene caught in crystal: the glass church, the green glass grass, and, to complete the microcosm, a skater on a pond.

'Sam? Sam, are you awake?'

'Ma?'

Grinning, rubbing his face, all angles, bones so sharp, Sam has grown so tall Moira has to look up at this giant son. He and his friends blot out the light nowadays. When they are gone Dan's house settles into its electrical routine. Returning, they bring the weather with them, leave doors open, Dan grumbles: his thermostats are deranged. Moira finds the young, Sam's friends, exasperating, enchanting, gentle, disclaiming need or hunger, yet ravenous.

13

It strikes her that just lately Sam has stopped bringing his friends home. In fact, except for Kate's son Donny, Moira has no idea who they are.

Sam has been sleeping as usual in underpants and a sweater (a T-shirt in summer) and stands wrapped in his duvet.

Are you all right? Are you happy? Moira would like to ask, but at some moment she cannot pin down it became impossible to ask that kind of question. Their relationship is amicable, tends to be jokey, but her huge son holds her politely at arm's length: thus far and no further. Kate always says: you're so lucky with Sam, you don't know. Kate's Donny is the same age and heading for trouble Moira judges. Privately, Moira considers that Kate watches Donny too much, she is looking for trouble and so will probably get it. Aids, drugs, suicide, extinction at the hands of the wild men of the Middle East: there are so many monsters in the forest nowadays. Name them and they'll come running.

But there was always despair, wasn't there? Youth is not so much to be envied – it has always been awful in one way or another, to be young.

Yet there is something different now?

'I've got to go out. There's a pizza in the freezer. You'll be all right?'

'Fine.'

The blind is down. Sam lives by electric light. Mugs all over the floor. Video cassettes almost all years old. Sam haunts video sales. *Deathstar*; *Alien*; *Sex, Lies and Videotape*; *The Deer Hunter* – Sam must have seen that twenty times. Moira realises that most of Sam's films date back to his childhood. Yet surely he is too young for nostalgia?

'It's been snowing. I think it's stopped now. It'll be clear by this afternoon, I expect. Why don't you see Donny?'

(Moira can hear her own voice from years ago, cheerful, competent: why don't you go out and play with Donny? That was when they lived in University Row and the children were always in one garden or another. In summer they ran naked under the hose and the wives were young then and lounged, gossiping, in the sun or the shade, knowing that the children

14

were safe in the garden. The women talked and watched the children squeal and jump and fall on the grass. Sometimes the hose made a rainbow. The foliage was lush. The women were in their first marriages then. A lot has changed, that at that time seemed immutable.)

Sam scratches his chest: his waking-up ritual.

'Ma. We don't play snowballs any more.'

'I think Kate's worried about Donny. That's all.'

'What Donny does is his own business.'

'Of course. Well.'

'It's all right. Honestly.'

'Yes.'

Sam waits until he hears the door shut, the car start after a couple of tries. Still he waits a moment. She could be back to fetch something she has forgotten. Lately, he has noticed, she is always going somewhere, coming back, making lists, in perpetual motion. They seem to need that, a reason to leave before they can come home. As if they were expiating something.

Now he can pee, which he does with a gasp of relief. He always holds out as long as he can, rather than quit the warmth of the bed.

Still wrapped in the duvet, Sam makes his way down the open stairs. (He remembers, when he was a child they put a gate at the top and he would crouch at the gate watching them move around the undivided spaces below. Or Sam thinks he remembers that. Yet surely they were still in University Row when he was so small he needed a gate? He must have been about seven when they came here. Perhaps the gate was for Lucy, though she couldn't get far by herself then. Except once, into the pool, when she drowned.)

While the kettle is coming to the boil, Sam goes to the row of switches under the stairs and turns up the thermostat. When Dan comes in he will turn it down.

Sam ignores the percolator and makes instant coffee, black, smothers two wodges of bread with peanut butter. The telephone rings. Sam pauses, goes to Moira's desk and switches off the telephone. He makes a quick survey of her desk. Heaps of books. Red file: empty. She's forgotten her cigarettes but she won't come back for them now. No other clues. A couple of hairpins.

He can hear the telephone still ringing upstairs and downstairs in the kitchen. He makes a round of the house unplugging it in the living area and in the kitchen. Upstairs he does the same in their bedroom. Here the colour scheme is blue duvet, grey walls and that insane 6 foot by 6 foot oil Dan's so proud of. Mostly black and white, just a fleck of red near the bottom right-hand corner. That's the only bit he likes – the red.

Not much sign of her here. The bedroom always smells of him. Not aftershave or sweat exactly – a male smell that faintly alarmed Sam when he was young. Still does. He and Donny discussed this once when they were about ten and left alone in the house (or it might have been the other house). They inspected the undersheet with their noses. Donny said it was like dog or horse, and for a week they'd talk about dogs and horses, a kind of joke private conversation, the signal for thumping each other and yelling with laughter. They sniffed their own armpits in a spirit of research. Dogs! Horses! Yip!

One wall of their bedroom is mirror. Sam opens his mouth and bares his teeth. Yellow. Grrr. He licks the fur.

Sometime he'll have to get down to hygiene. A teeth-scrape. Dan uses an electric toothbrush: that's the signal for the house waking up, even before he pees Dan stands stark naked working on his teeth. (Horses have big yellow teeth.)

Sam could do with a shave too. Tomorrow. Or grow a beard.

Tomorrow he will decide who he is. Not that they'll notice. That's the weird thing about this weird house: you can see everything but no one seems to see anyone else.

He looks up at his ceiling. Might paint it black. He crouches on his haunches in front of the video and keeps his finger on fast-forward. He kills the sound. The gooks have hauled Nick out of the bamboo cage, they spin the

16

pistol and hold their guns on him. On the other side of the table Robert de Niro is saying: Go on Nick, I love you. Fast-forward again. And again. The deer stands in the snow in the blue light.

Dan Frankland sits in his osteopath's waiting-room. He sits in the ergonomic black leather chair but his lumbar region still complains. His leg answers. The old wound sustained neither in battle nor sport nor even the pursuit of love. Women, girls, are attracted by his limp, ask with wide eyes how he won it. Sometimes Daniel can spin it out for days, weeks, but they always get to know in the end.

Dan Frankland tore his Achilles' tendon ten years ago.

Dan Frankland slipped on an apple one autumn.

From where he sits (wincing), Dan can see through glass, Birgit, Horseman's receptionist, watering the monstera in the small outer office. When he slipped on the apple she consoled him. Birgit has kissed his heel. Out of hours they have lain together on the very couch towards which Dan is now hobbling.

Birgit loosed her breasts and her golden hair. She kissed his heel and rode him and upon the moment put her finger to his lips. No, she said, no talk. She refused to meet him anywhere but here. Dan knew nothing of her life. He saw her once shopping in Tesco's and was astonished by her housewifely manner, her gold ring, her laden trolley.

Last month she said: I have a husband, you know.

Smiling.

He is not so well.

If you need to talk you can see me.

But they never had talked.

This morning Dan is jealous of the monstera but Horseman is talking about the weather, about nothing in particular, as he always does while he probes the tender spots, manipulates without warning.

'Here?'

'There.'

17

Dan is on his face, forked, vulnerable creature. Do women feel like this, giving birth?

'And how is Moira?'

'We're having the party as usual. You'll come?'

'There, is it, then?'

If this couch could speak. If you knew.

Osteopaths are like fashionable dentists nowadays. Piped Mozart. This morning Horseman's fingers on the spine are cold and, as ever, precise. Dan dreams of Horseman. He dreams that Horseman is drawing out his soul, manipulating it. There, that's better now.

'Mozart?'

'Piano concerto.'

'Very appropriate.' I am a piano, thinks Dan.

'I think we have a little knot here? The family?'

'Fine. Hell!' But it works. It still works. 'You ought to be a piano tuner.'

'That's what my mother did. My father was a wrestler.'

'So?' Dan wraps a towel round his shanks. Horseman sits, looks at his notes, looks up.

'How is life in general?'

I am dying. My soul is grazed by daily living.

'You see, you are not a young man. At your age it is no longer a matter of the primary injury. The body is like a family. What happens to one affects the whole.'

'You mean the hip bone is connected to the thigh bone.'

Give up, you'll never get a laugh out of Horseman. He is the only one who never thought the fall on the apple was funny.

'You could say that.' Horseman nods. 'Though it is more a matter of dislocation.' There is a spark in Horseman's flat eye. 'That is to say, are you limping much lately?'

'I am limping.'

'Well. So you see – the limp deforms the whole body. The leg. The lumbar region. Tell me, have you any pains in the neck? Headaches?'

'Not yet. Pleasure to come.'

'If you continue to limp.'

Dan pauses, pulling on his trousers. There is a screen behind

which, presumably, Horseman's female patients undress and
dress.
 'And how do I stop limping?'
 'There is no physiological reason why you should. Limp.
The tendon is mended.'
 'You think I'd limp if I didn't have to?'
 'You say Moira's well?'
 'What's Moira got to do with it?'
Horseman taps his teeth with his pen. If birds had teeth
they would be like that: very small, small as milk teeth.
Except for starlings – they would have fangs.
 'There is a lot of stress nowadays. Distress.'
 'If you're talking about my sex life, it's fine, thank you.'
 'You would be amazed. Especially the mid-life distress.
Quite crippling. There is only so much I can do. The fear.
I have the impression that people are afraid. Thank you,
Birgit.'
 Dan is dressed now. It is eleven o'clock and Birgit has
brought in Horseman's coffee. As she bends to put it on his
desk, it is clear that beneath the clinical white coat she wears
nothing but her bra. How has Dan never noticed before that
there is the faintest golden growth above her upper lip? Oh,
my downy love.
 Dan is sweating. He had forgotten: Horseman always
keeps up the heat for his naked patients yet he never sweats
himself. Outside the world is bitter, the traffic clogged by the
weather, people walk knifed in half inside their weather-wear:
lumbar distress. From here one can see a single university
spire scrawled against a white sky. In here is a tropic zone.
 Birgit is back in her office. She is wiping the giant leaves
of the monstera with milk.
 Afraid?
 Horseman stands as Dan makes to leave. Favoured patient.
Steady source of income, rather. On my dislocated bones,
over the years, he could have gone twice round the world,
club class.
 Standing, Dan has the advantage of a good three inches
and strong shoulders. He could pick up Horseman and snap
him in half. If it weren't for his back.

19

'So what do you think they're afraid of?'

'They don't know. If they knew there would not be the distress.'

As simple as that? Halfway down the stairs, Dan wonders. Then he remembers to limp.

TWO

*I*t is eleven o'clock. Moira is later than she meant to be but the snow has held up the traffic. Dan has taken the Volvo and Moira always finds the estate car heavy. But she manages and by eleven thirty, after all, she is drinking coffee with Kate in University Row.

The hug. 'I'm so glad you came. Oh, you feel so cold.'

'It is cold.'

Kate Summerson looks about sixteen. That never changes. So tiny, so skinny, the cap of black hair without a trace of grey, the enormous eyes. She has been mistaken for Donny's sister (poor Donny, he hates that). All the year round she wears washed-out jeans, sweatshirts like her son's and in winter loose sweaters, sometimes Donny's. For special occasions she favours the layered look.

When Moira has taken off her jacket Kate tugs her by the hands.

'Come on. By the stove. Oh, your poor hands! Where's the car?'

'I parked it behind the library. I thought this road would be bad.'

Kate nods, fusses with coffee.

'It's because we're a cul-de-sac. They never bother to clear it. Are the snow-ploughs out?'

'Not yet.'

Moira sinks into the big chair by the stove (Victorian done over, so many years ago). In this same chair, now half collapsed, Kate, when they were neighbours in University Row, had been sitting, feet curled under, when she announced her pregnancy. Here she had suckled Donny and Poppy, told Moira – her eyes brimming before they

21

spilled over – of Howard's first infidelity. That is, the first infidelity she knew of. Moira had thought it might break her – certainly the second or the third – but Kate, telling all, so helpless-seeming, confiding, had survived. Survives.

Through the arch that divides the kitchen from the muddly front room, Moira can see the indoor plants that (like the children) survive Kate's slap-dash attentions: passionate concern one moment, forgetfulness the next, followed by repentance and over-watering. And beyond, the door to the garden, which in the snow seems smaller, a sad monochrome.

The coffee is awful but Moira warms her hands on the mug.

'I was remembering. Trying to remember. When we all came here. The gardens in summer were lovely, weren't they?'

Visibly, Kate relaxes a little. She settles like a young girl on the floor by the stove, unclenches. She puts a hand to the back of her neck, kneads, dips her head and then looks up, smiling.

'Yes. Oh yes, I do remember! You do too? Maybe I think about it too much. And I think I've invented some of it. The weather can't have been so good all the time. I remember Donny and Sam playing under the hose. And the garden. I could grow anything in those days. Everything seemed easy in those summers – the children, cooking, gardening. D'you remember the fig? Howard said we never had one. But there was a fig, wasn't there?'

Moira nods. 'Yes. There was even some fruit one year. We were determined to eat it. Someone got ill. Then it got too big – it was undermining the house or something. But I can't remember who cut it down? You know, I miss it here.'

There is a dangerous shine to Kate's eyes.

'Oh, I miss you too, so much! How awful, I nearly forgot. How's your mother?'

'I haven't been yet. I don't think she particularly wants to see me. And I still feel I've got to go. Crazy, I suppose. The dutiful daughter thing, you know. I could never abandon her even if Dan told me to.' Moira rummages in her bag. No cigarettes. Kate doesn't smoke. 'You know that expression

American sociologists use? The kin-keepers. They mean women.'

'Oh, Lord! Oh no!'

'Yes.'

Moira thinks, we can still laugh. That must be something. She realises how much she relishes the company of women. Women can speak to each other in a dolphin language, mind to mind communication, without words. Kate never mentions Lucy.

She remembers: 'I used to wonder what it would be like – living in a University town but not belonging to the University. If it would matter.'

'Has it?'

'To Dan a bit, I think. People always assumed he was a don, then he had to tell them he was an architect. Maybe that's why he needed to build that house – Dan's ground.'

Kate nods.

'I can understand that. Everyone needs their own ground. Habitat.'

'You'll stay here?' Moira asks. She means, if Howard has gone for good.

Kate's eyes grow even larger.

'I don't think I could bear to move.' Kate can weep and talk and not know that she is weeping. Now she is at the kitchen counter spreading crackers with cottage cheese, filling two beakers with white wine and tears.

Kate's marmalade cat stirs from his place in front of the stove, stretches, measures the leap to Moira's lap and flicks the tip of his tail.

'Hello, Mouser.'

'He doesn't like smokers.'

'I'm not smoking.'

'He can smell it.'

'Sniffer cat.' Moira grins. Kate has never smoked. When Howard gave it up she tried to make the house a no-smoking zone. Moira continued to smoke and Kate rushed to open the windows, made a drama of finding a cracked saucer for an ashtray. Tacit negotiations followed and détente was achieved. Now Moira smokes here and Kate no longer winces every time a cigarette is lit. On the other hand Moira rations herself, sometimes does without altogether, and always empties the ashtray and washes it before she leaves.

Kate eats like a squirrel. Holds her cracker between her fingers and snaps off the corner as if the big bad wolf were waiting at the foot of the tree. Moira sees them all at a picnic, teasing Kate as she fills the little pouches of her cheeks with grapes, Howard feeding her, Moira leaning back against Dan, all of them in the sun (where were the children?), willows, water. Years ago.

Moira sees that Kate is watching for an opening so she might just as well give it to her.

'Have you really tried to talk to Howard? I mean, will he talk?'

Kate takes a deep breath.

'You'd never believe it. He says I ought to see a shrink.'

'Oh, Katie, no, that's insane.'

'Perhaps I am, though not in the way he means. I want him back. Is that crazy? I mean, whatever he's done, whatever he's doing. Any terms. He says I'm a masochist, I make him feel guilty.'

'Has he ever thought he might be guilty himself? If he didn't cheat there'd be no guilt.'

'But then if he cheats there must be a reason.'

'Katie, we've been through this a hundred times.'

A tremulous smile.

'Of course, you and Dan. D'you know how lucky you are?'

'Yes, I do. But Katie, there's no such thing as the perfect marriage.'

There is always the locked drawer. Even as she speaks Moira brushes away intimations, images, signals. Well, Dan's been tired lately, a bad patch, his back. Horseman's a bad influence – he encourages his phobias.

Moira looks out at the small garden. She can't leave Kate like this. There is too much history between them.

'Remember when Dan built the pool? Even before the

24

house. That summer? Wasn't it heaven?' Smiling, through half-closed eyelids, she can call it up: the gold, the green, the incredible shattering blue of the bland-faced pool. Someone had brought champagne: the first bottle a libation to the god of the pool. They had drunk the rest. There was no house then – just the foundations which sketched the shape within which rooms would rise. The machines dozed while Dan broke the surface of the water waving his trunks, and then they all stripped off and swam naked, shocking the children.

Moira asks Kate: 'Who else was there? That first time we used the pool?'

'Judith and Morris Kraft.'

Oh, yes. They had known the Krafts on and off, though not well, for years. Morris was something to do with the University, Judith a psychologist. Of all the crowd who dated back to those old days, Moira had known Judith least well, yet felt she might like her best. She might have known her better but Judith had helped Sam professionally at the clinic in the difficult time after the accident, and somehow that had made Moira shy of her. A little jealous perhaps? What had Sam told her that he couldn't tell me? What reason is there ever that two people who might have been intimates never take that step? Say the word? And having failed, it becomes more difficult.

Now she remembers that first time at the pool, Judith Kraft floating serenely on a mattress, her hair fanning out behind her like seaweed. She turned out to have surprisingly large breasts, out of keeping somehow with her normal air of self-possession, smiling common sense. Morris Kraft, sitting demurely at the shallow end, was sipping from his glass and smoking a cigar. Short, nearly bald, yet wearing, it seemed, a vest of thick, curled, black dog-like hair from the top of his sternum to his underwater root.

Breast-stroking at the deep end, Moira had felt her ankles seized, then as she thrashed, Dan's head broke the water and they were laughing, loving as they often did that summer in the pool. Dan in the water was amazing, a marine centaur, rejoicing in evolution reversed. He could swim three lengths underwater.

Moira feels sure she knows which evening it was that she conceived towards the end of summer. It strikes her as miraculous that she conceived Lucy underwater. Then the first shadows reached for them, long-fingered, and drove them from the pool.

Since the accident memory has proved dangerous. There are times when it must be blocked.

Kate is still wrapt in remembrance.

She is saying: 'Do you remember what big boobs Judith had?'

Moira laughs, sighs, gets up, pulls on her jacket, kisses Kate's cheek, tasting salt.

'Hold on, love. Ring you.'

In the short time Moira has been at Kate's the air has frozen into a greyness. Moira buys cigarettes. In the estate car she turns on the heater. Denied the precious Volvo, Sam is allowed to drive the estate car and as the temperature increases Moira is aware of the slightly acid smell that attaches also to his bedroom (she had thought after puberty this would vanish but it didn't, the boy smell). There is the feel of something sticky on the wheel and on the floor where once one would have crunched plastic toys underfoot there is a dustbinful of discarded wrappings from chocolate bars, crisp bags, an old movie magazine; in the back more crumpled paper, jeans cut down to swim in, a plastic slip-slop sandal, a broken snorkel, a frisbee, the yellowed mattress upon which, after an outing, the children used to quarrel and shout and droop, curl finally into sleep as soft and suddenly as exhausted puppies. The detritus of summer. Time. (And now does Sam bring his girls here? Do they love on that mattress?) Sam doesn't smoke but the pull-out ashtray is full. There are even stamped-out butts on the floor. In the glove-pocket more rubbish and a broken earring, one of those bulldog clip hair things girls wear nowadays: plastic in the shape of blue butterfly wings.

Are they clues to a life, such tokens? How does he live?

26

Can't empty the ashtray here. Moira closes it with difficulty, waits until she is on the road, winds the window open a crack and throws out her cigarette butt. The main road from the centre of town to the hospital is beginning to freeze again, the radio warns of black ice, plays a jingle and interviews a woman who saves dogs. There is a crackle. She sounds unstable, or it could be that she is nervous of radio. She says that she walks the streets at night looking for dogs. Another jingle and chirpy advice on precautions against hypothermia. Moira snaps off the radio and slows up behind a heavy lorry. The weather has brought an early, false dusk. Lights have been lit, fires crackle in the Edwardian houses behind clumps of dirty laurel. As Moira looks a woman in a red dress comes to a window, turns to speak to someone in the room, draws a curtain. Secret lives.

There is a hold-up. The traffic is one-way and, winding down the window to peer out, Moira sees a flashing red light, orange bollards, a police-car. She has a slight headache. The yip-yip of an ambulance going away. The traffic moves again. Thanks to the University, until recently the hospital has been well funded. On the edge of town, it has grown, claiming a little more land each year. Dan worked on it – his biggest contract. Every so often a new cube is added, like a child's building set. As Moira approaches, the metal sky leaks a sickly lemon sun.

In the hospital car park Moira bumps into Judith Kraft, leaving. She is a handsome woman. She wears a blue suede coat, ankle-length. There is sleet on her grey-streaked chestnut hair.

They both laugh. In the fading light they nearly collide. Then both say, almost in the same breath: I meant to ring you.

Moira smiles. 'Funny, I was just thinking about you. I was going to ask you both to the party, Christmas Eve.'

'We'd love that. How's Sam?'

'Fine. Sam seems fine.'

Judith nods.

'I'd meant to ring you to ask about your mother.'

'Oh, you know. The same. Tests.'

'It's difficult with parents. I remember.' Judith Kraft appears to be searching for the right words. Queer, Moira thinks, I never saw Judith as someone who might have problems of her own.

'I think,' Judith goes on, 'maybe nowadays we neglect the necessary rites? You know what I mean? It's a risk. It will be a strain for you.'

'Oh, well.'

Moira is about to leave when Judith says: 'Do you have a second?'

'Of course.'

'I've just been to see a girl in the psychiatric wing.'

'Your patient?'

'Not officially.' Judith half smiles, shrugs. 'In any case I'm not sure there's anything doctors can do for her. She's a sort of derelict. Tried to cut her wrists so she finished up here. It's a lot to ask but if you had a moment, I wonder if you'd just look in and see her. Her name's Minnie Flynn. She's what our dreadful trade calls non-cooperative. Don't give it another thought if you'd rather not. She might be very rude. Most likely she won't talk at all. In particular, she won't talk to doctors. But as far as we can make out she has no one in the world. Can you imagine?'

Moira shakes her head.

'I'll look in when I've seen Mother.'

'If you're really sure? I'd be grateful. And while your mother's like this, if there's anything I can do. If you want to talk. About anything.'

The sleet has stopped but the wind whirls around them, between them, parts them. Moira calls: Thank you. But her words blow away.

Inside the hospital colours are primary. White, with the arrows and doors to each unit red, dark blue, orange. Same colours for the synthetic floor covering which gives the impression of being cushioned. The nurses too wear white, soundless shoes.

Freda Collier: all that rage pinned under a white sheet. The

28

red blanket turned down. She doesn't look at the magazines Moira has brought.

'They don't know anything. They mess me about.'

Moira walks to the window.

'You get the sun here.' Oily pools of yellow on the white fields.

'I can't stay here. It's making me ill.'

'Sam and Dan send their love.'

'It's terrible for me in this place.'

'Yes, I know.'

Moira thinks, if I were not her daughter compassion would be easy. What is now anger was once vitality. I can see that. I can understand why this woman – who is still, in a wracked way, handsome – is angry. This rage may even be good for her. It doesn't matter what I feel. I am simply not the daughter she wanted but that is not my fault. So why do I feel guilty now? I can't sit still in this room.

'It's a beautiful view. D'you remember the snow scene? The paperweight? I still have it. I always loved it.'

'I looked for that in the flat. I couldn't find it.'

'No, Mother. You gave it to me years ago.' Steady, don't be upset, she's ill. Why do the hands of the wall-clock move so slowly?

Freda's fingers pull at the red blanket. Behind the eyes there is some tremendous mental effort. She has the expression of a child struggling for the words to get what it wants.

'Home. I want to. Go home.' A breathless rest then the eyelids open again. She speaks quite clearly. 'I want you to air the flat, order the milk and papers and take me home.'

'When you're better. Soon.' I sound like a bloody health visitor. The awful thing is, she means it. Entirely rationally. And why not? All they do is tests that seem to weaken her each time. We could make arrangements. I suppose I'm frightened that she couldn't manage, even with help, that in the end she would come to me.

'It's snowing.'

Freda says: 'I used to like snow. You know, the sun never suited me at all. I always stayed in the shade. I took good care of my skin. Did you say Sam was coming?'

29

'Yes. He promised. Very soon.'

She has forgotten already about going home. That's one mercy. There are long periods now (are they getting longer, more frequent?) when a hand seems to have been drawn across Freda's eyes and she looks at me in bewilderment as if I were a guest whose name she cannot remember. Then her face smooths with forgetfulness and she has the appearance of a girl lost, without tricks. Quite young. Her skin is still so fine and white, it has its own dry scent. Goodbye. I'll come again. Very soon.

Moira talks to the doctor. He is one of the younger ones who still have the capacity for concern. He'll lose that or crack up. With his white coat, white office and black desk, an infants' drawing pinned to his notice board is the only colour in the room. A green tree with stick arms like a scarecrow and big yellow sun with red rays.

The usual thing, Mrs Frankland. Your mother. Still waiting for results of tests. Crossed lines. All the same nowadays. Computers.

'Yes, I do understand. My husband has the same problem.'

Actually, I don't want to know. You might guess from my appearance that I am supposed to be the sensible one in the family. Moira copes. I do usually, I suppose because I am conditioned to respond as expected. Except for one period which is a blank in my memory. Just lately, however, I have had some images you might call mad.

'Of course. Your husband built a good hospital. Gone down a bit, I'm afraid.'

'You'll let me know about the tests? I mean, if anything comes up.'

'You know the way out? Well, naturally you do.'

'Yes.'

'Was there something else, Mrs Frankland?'

'I wondered if I could see Minnie Flynn?'

'Minnie? You know her?'

'No. Judith Kraft from the clinic suggested it.'

'Well. Yes, there's no reason she should not have visitors. Officially, there's no reason why she should still be here. But you know the situation? You shouldn't expect much?'

'Yes.'

'In that case.' The doctor stood.

'It's all right. I know my way. The red arrow?'

In the narrow room with the door wedged open, the girl is sitting on her neatly made bed. She might always have been sitting there. Her posture is that of a statue. She sits with her hands palms upwards in her lap, looking at her hands, her shoulders slumped. Frozen life, Moira thinks. She takes a deep breath.

'My name's Moira Frankland. Dr Kraft suggested. I didn't know what you'd like so I brought you some oranges.'

'Yes.'

Since Minnie makes no move, Moira puts the bag of oranges on the bed. Her long, pale hair is fastened with an elastic band. Clean. The hospital will have seen to that.

Moira feels too warm, too big, too alive. She sits in the single red chair, tries not to look at the girl's thin, bandaged wrists.

The door and the chair are red, the walls are white. There is a poster of a wind-surfer on a blue wave in a brilliant sun. At the tip the wave is creaming to white, about to break. No mirror. Well, there wouldn't be. The glass. Blu-tacked to the wall is a small painting: a red sky takes up the top third of the paper, the rest is a jagged mountain range, black.

'Did you do that?'

For the first time the girl looks at Moira then at the picture.

'They make me do painting. Then they ask me stupid questions.'

Moira nods. Minnie stands and walks to the window, one hand to her mouth, chewing her finger-nails. She has the usual half-starved look. An Irish accent. 'Perhaps you'd rather not be disturbed?'

Moira feels foolish.

'That's all right.' Minnie hasn't even opened the bag of oranges. Her face is still blank but there is a struggle of some kind behind her eyes, perhaps to speak. Poor child. She really is only a child. 'Are you a doctor?'

'Oh, no.' Apparently the right answer. 'I was just here so I came to see if you wanted anything.'

'I'm not supposed to be here.'

'Yes, I know.'

'I'm not mad. I didn't do anything mad. They don't know where to put me.'

'Books? Clothes? Anything like that. I could bring you anything.'

'All I want is a room but they won't let me go on my own.'

'You've got a radio. Do you listen to it?'

'I like telly. You can see it in the lounge, they said I could, but they make me sick.'

'Who makes you sick, Minnie?'

'Min. That's my name. All those old cripples. Some of them are dying. They give me the creeps.'

'Yes. I can understand that. Well.' With the light on, the window is a strict black square, alarming. Moira feels shaky (snow-nerves again) and is seized by the most urgent need to get home before she is snowed out. Before she makes promises she cannot fulfil.

'I could come again. If you'd like me to?'

The girl looks her full in the face. She has that very thin skin that goes with her colouring, as if she might bruise easily (bleed). In summer she would have freckles.

'If you want to. I wouldn't mind.'

'Well.' Moira stands.

'It's snowing.'

The girl touches the window. On the other side of the glass a single one of the many-falling flakes has drifted and stuck.

Following the green arrow for out, Moira remembers that in its day this was a model hospital. In the *Architectural Review* and circles in which such matters are spoken of respectfully. It was fashionable then. It is still spoken of with nostalgia for a certain time. Since then so many cubes have been added it resembles an airport complex. Like an international airport it has its own chapel and mortuary. Even when Dan said it had reached its limits a kind of parthenogenesis continued. His first concept was lost in a sprawl checked only by the loss of funding. The University which had largely subsidised it is now begging for money itself. Several wards have had to be closed.

Dan can never quite detach himself from this place. He is worried about deterioration, materials that have developed mysterious illnesses. He spends far too much time trying to raise money. He worries about the air-conditioning. If there were an outbreak of Legionnaire's disease it is possible he might be sued. Moira thinks not. After all, he is not responsible for upkeep. But he won't talk about it. He won't see a lawyer.

In a survey a year or two ago it was found that patients who could look out upon trees were the first to recover. Freda could see fields, if they were not under snow. I like snow.

Well, the hospital works more or less, that's the main thing. Or if there is a mortal flaw no one has detected it. Or if they have, they have not reported it. The fabric of the hospital is like our house. Our marriage. The marriage which is between us. If you were to ask me, I'd say it works so well I haven't looked at it for years, Dan and I and our marriage. It's fine, thank you. Quite famous. Surely?

There is the Christmas display already in Foggerton's lighted window, then the town, the suburbs and the road out, home. Moira backs the estate car to make way for a sudden apparition: a tall yellow snow-plough. There could have been a collision. As it is, the windscreen has to be wiped clean of the snow the plough has thrown up.

The opaque black windows of the house give no sign of life.

Moira has to park outside the garage. The drive is blocked. But she's home. She's thankful. She ducks against the slanting snow, taking deep breaths of cold, and calls out as she opens the door.

'Anyone home?'

33

THREE

*S*am has left his door ajar. He is propped on his bed with Barney, the dog they got him after the accident, as if a dog were a person. But he likes Barney's ruggy pelt and cheerful grin. They thought Barney would be good for him and in a way he was, though not the way they meant.

That was around the time Sam just didn't want to go out much and stopped going to school for a bit (that is, he let Dan drop him at school but didn't go in). They found out in the end and Sam was sent to talk to that woman therapist friend of Moira's. They seemed embarrassed. Sam didn't mind but he couldn't think of much to say to Dr Kraft. He used to invent things but she was nice, she wasn't stupid, she probably guessed, so then he'd just sit in Dr Judith Kraft's office until it was time to go home. Of course, he was only a kid then. He did a few paintings for her because she asked but he never knew what happened to them or if they meant anything. He did like her though. Once or twice in the years since, passing her office, he'd thought of looking in, just in a friendly way. But there didn't seem much point. It would have been peculiar, talking to Dr Kraft in a room full of toys and children's paintings.

It must have been Dr Kraft who suggested the dog because Barney arrived towards the end of the time Sam was seeing her. He imagines now that Barney was intended to make up for him being an only child after Lucy died. They said the dog was his responsibility, it was *his* dog, he must look after it, which was fairly stupid because he was too young then to look after anything. Anyhow if you have a sister or a brother you don't have to feed them and clean up their messes. Dan never liked the idea of the dog. Sam remembered

34

him yelling once when Barney had made a puddle in his study and after that Moira did the feeding and the training and the clearing up.

Barney can more or less look after himself now as long as he's fed so everything's much easier. He goes off alone quite a lot but when they're both in, he's with Sam, he sleeps in Sam's room. It's funny how he's really fond of that dog now. That is to say, when he thinks about it Sam is afraid of Barney's death.

Sam has left the door open because it's about time one of them came home and he's beginning to feel hungry. He can always tell by the sound of the car and the door shutting if it's his father, who will go straight for a drink. If it's Moira she'll chew up the gravel manoeuvring the estate car while Dan parks the Volvo tenderly, whatever mood he's in. His mother will call out and then go to the kitchen. She'll get a drink from the white wine in the fridge and stub out her cigarette if Sam comes down, so he always gives her long enough to smoke half a cigarette while she decides what to convey from the deep-freeze to the microwave. He wishes she'd give up because he doesn't want her to die. He tells himself they're all dying one way or another but hardly anyone smokes nowadays.

His mother is calling. On the remote control Sam summons the local oracle, Delphi, and the message is presented on the screen: Due to weather the lecture on the greenhouse effect is cancelled.

'Ma?'

'Spaghetti all right?'

'Great.'

So she's going to cook tonight. To Sam's certain knowledge there is no spaghetti in the freezer, she'll have to make it fresh. He and Barney and Donny ate it a couple of weeks ago. It was Donny's idea to give some to the dog and eat his own at floor-level from a bowl. Barney sniffed the garlic, gave Donny that stiff-necked look he can do and went under the table where he sat with his big head on his paws while Donny barked and pushed the bowl round the floor with his nose. In the end Barney accepted a couple of meatballs but he didn't approve of Donny nowadays, though they used to get on well enough when they were all young. Sam tends to agree with him. Sometimes he thinks Donny is really crazy.

He switches from Delphi to the national news. A lot of stuff about the weather. Helicopters dropping whatever sheep eat. Dead sheep in snowdrifts. More snow somewhere else. Men talking or pretending to talk for the camera round a round table. Sam flips off the sound. The men go on talking.

There'll be nothing to eat for an hour at least. If his mother's cooking they'll have to wait for Dan and he's always late.

Sam slides out from under Barney's head and crouches secretly as he did as a child to look through the landing rail. In this crazy house you can see from here straight down into the living area and the kitchen. You know what's cooking all over the house but best from here as the smells rise. She's standing at the stove stirring a sauce with one hand and smoking with the other. Down two steps is the dining area though when they're alone they usually eat at the kitchen table. Up one level from the kitchen is the living area, in darkness now, but Sam can just make out the low sofa where one summer afternoon he saw them making love, if that's what they were making. All he knows is that it frightened him and he didn't know why. He didn't want to tell Donny about it even though they were very interested in sex at the time. He never did tell Donny or Dr Kraft or anyone.

Moira is stirring the tomato sauce. She puts her cigarette down in the ashtray and takes another sip of white wine. Cooking, she feels better. Getting together the ingredients, adding the bay leaf just as the sauce reaches the right viscosity. It is like a spell and, shifting her weight from one foot to another she runs over her unsatisfactory, vaguely troubling day, images she has not been able to interpret, put away, behind her. She reaches for the blind to shut out the night. At just the moment the big yellow magical eyes of Dan's Volvo rake the darkness, point first the feathery tips of the black conifers and then in an hallucinatory second before he

36

eases the car so considerately from the curve of the drive into the garage, show Dan the beautiful snowflakes idling, wondering, and finally in their slow obedience to gravity, settling in the empty pool.

'I have to go to town tomorrow,' Dan says.
'Yes?'
Moira smiles, serves the spaghetti with more ceremony than usual. She's even grated fresh parmesan and put together a green salad: chicory from the crisper. She's up to something, Sam judges.

Dan had one if not two whiskies between coming in and sitting at the table. Since he put a door on his office he's in there most evenings working. Or drinking. Gradually the open plan is breaking down: a door here, a lock there. Moira knows he keeps Scotch in the office and sees no reason why he shouldn't. It strikes her that only once in the whole of their marriage has she been aware that Dan was drunk and there was reason for that.

'Will the trains be running?'
'If not, the motorway will be clear.'
Abruptly the image is returned to her: the apparition of the tall yellow snow-plough. She doesn't care for Chianti but she's opened a bottle tonight because Dan does. She is drinking a little more than usual herself.

'Should you drive? How's your back?'
Dan grimaces.
'I saw Horseman today. He said I should stop limping. But the Volvo's fine. It's the only time my back's really comfortable.'
'He gives me the creeps.'
'Horseman?'
The portable television slung in the corner of the kitchen is talking quietly. Greenland devoured by sheep, experts reveal. Link between sliced bread and schizophrenia suspected. Eden Tower, another, almost the last, of the high-rise blocks, sways under the cold sky, for an extraordinary second or so, hesitates before it falls. Moira is reminded.
'The Ridgely contract – what's happening?'

37

'Tied up. Pretty well.'

'But that's marvellous.'

Even as she speaks Moira remembers a queer little scene just after Dan got the contract for housing at a government research plant. With the Summersons, they had driven out in the spring and looked over the acres the project would swallow, the waving grass, the fallow land. Then that evening there was the barbecue for Howard Summerson's birthday, when Kate had drunk too much and timid, vulnerable Kate had screamed at Dan: Killer! Just because it was an MoD contract. Howard had slapped her face before she stopped weeping and that had been the end of the party. And Kate had rung three days running to apologise. None of them has spoken of it since. Anyway, the Summersons are no longer a family now, though Moira guesses that Howard will be back.

Moira stacks the plates in the dishwasher, makes coffee. She thinks of Kate, who has a dishwasher but won't use it. She is electrically incompetent and doesn't seem to care.

'I was at the hospital today.'

'Mmn.'

Either Dan or Sam has turned up the sound on the television. News again. Dan hates to miss the news, he'll see it three times in one evening. And the weather, as if he were a sailor or a farmer.

Moira sits at the table, lights a cigarette, waits for the news to finish.

'D'you think those Irish talks will come to anything?'

Dan shrugs. Barney ambles into the kitchen, checks his family and gives a half wag.

'I saw a girl called Minnie Flynn at the hospital. Weird name, isn't it. Judith Kraft asked me to.'

Dan has turned off the television and is looking at the paper.

'What is she? This Minnie Flynn?'

'A sort of waif really. Cut her wrists. I don't know if there were drugs. Anyway, she has no family, no one seems to care. The hospital's got her but they don't know what to do with her. The psychiatric ward is full and it's mostly geriatric. I thought I might bring her over one day?'

38

'Why not?' Dan isn't listening, Sam judges.

'You wouldn't mind?'

'Why should I?'

So that's what she's up to, thinks Sam.

'And I saw Kate today.'

He pulls a face.

'I saw Howard.'

She stubs out her cigarette murderously, grinding it to death. There is something tense about the angle of her neck. She sits up very straight, still killing that cigarette, not looking at Dan. An attitude Sam recognises. Smile a bit tight.

'You used to be very fond of Kate,' she says.

'I am still fond of Kate. And Howard.'

'They're our oldest friends.'

'So they are.'

'You remember University Row?' she asks, not really asking.

'Who could forget it?'

'The Summersons were very kind to us.'

'Everyone was very kind to everyone, if I remember. Some even kinder than others.'

'What do you mean by that?'

'Musical beds. And Howard wasn't the only one.'

Dan's eyes glint as he tops up the glasses.

'Mmn. You might be right.'

A crackle of danger but she's a good general. She knows when to stop. She smiles straight at Dan, yawns and lets go, her hand absently easing the top of her spine, where the day has gathered into a knot. There was a programme Sam saw about a disease you get from dogs that deforms your whole skeleton and makes your skull swell. That must be horrible.

'So how's Howard?' she says.

'Penitent. Poor old Howard.'

'Yes. I'm sorry for them both.'

Sam looks at his parents and wonders, since they are known to be happily married, why they seem to be talking in code nowadays. Perhaps they always did and he's only just noticed. Donny says he's lucky that they don't have rows like his, that's really murder, but sometimes Sam thinks the way they talk, as if they were always dodging something, is a kind of running row. It might be better if they did fight, so long as he was not required to take sides.

They both look older this winter but that might be because his grandmother is dying. If she is. Dying.

Dan stands. His back nearly jack-knifes him. The fiend Horseman says basically it's an evolutionary problem. When *homo erectus* first stood up straight over one million years ago he ceased to be an ape and began to get back trouble, because the spine never quite caught up. At least, that's one theory.

'I'll just check the pool,' Dan says, as if he had not said the same thing every night this winter. He is worried about the frost.

'Well, Sambo?'

Dan's hand rests briefly on the nape of his son's neck, when what he wants is to draw the boy to him – weep perhaps – flesh to his flesh. But that's all he ever does. Well, Sambo, he says, and limps out to check the pool where once – it seems to Dan a hundred years ago – that same hand cradled his son's chin, supported his belly so that he would swim, not sink. Was it like that for the first reptiles, their small lungs pumping in terror in the dangerous element of air?

Barney follows Dan out. Moira takes the last of the wine upstairs to the bedroom. At the window she can make out nothing but pitch black night, until Sam on his way out of the kitchen snaps on the garden light, and there at the edge of the pool are Dan and Barney, the man and the dog: a tall shape and something that might be his shadow. Then the dog-shadow detaches itself and the man takes a first cautious step into the drained and frozen pool.

The snow has held off, the roads are clear but the weather seems to be waiting. Danger of black ice. Sam holds the joint to his mouth, pretends to inhale and passes it on. He tried that when he and Donny were twelve but all it did was make him dizzy. Donny makes a great business of it, holding it between his second finger and thumb, closing his eyes while he sucks

40

it in but Sam's fairly sure that most of the way Donny goes on about smoking and popping pills is for show, like a lot of the things he does.

'Man!' breathes Donny, throws back his shaved head and stretches his long legs. He still wears the Doc Martens boots and all the gear as if he'd got stuck at fourteen or so. Sam came out in trainers because that was what he happened to be wearing when he decided to drop in on the Black Hole, and a sweater that smells of Barney. Donny surveys Sam from beneath half-closed lids. 'Where you been then?'

His voice, except when he forgets, is a high-pitched croak with a sort of whine at the back of it. Sam can't quite remember when Donny started talking like this but when you've known someone long enough perhaps you don't notice when they change. He himself feels he changes almost every day. He never knows who he is going to be when he wakes up. Sometimes he thinks he's no one at all: just a speck like the spot you get when you have looked at the sun and closed your eyes and opened them again and the spot's still there. Heavy Metal helps usually, even though it's old stuff nowadays. Or any other kind of music loud enough. He doesn't go to concerts any more but he likes it in the Black Hole, though he could be growing out of it. He's beginning to feel a bit like an old man here. The girls seem to be getting younger. Some of them can't be more than fourteen, even twelve.

'Nowhere much.'

They sit companionably, their backs to the wall, their knees under their chins. That's one thing about having known someone for ever – you don't have to talk. A few of the old crowd drift up to pay their respects. At some time Sam can't quite recall Donny became pack leader. Most likely he simply decided he was and everyone else fell in with the idea. The pack, however, is now on the edge of disintegration. There are those like Sam still hanging on at school, those who have gone on to the Poly or the sixth-form college, even one or two already at the University. As things are nowadays, no one expects a job for certain. Sally – with whom Sam nearly lost his virginity this summer – is working in the

41

supermarket. Tiger (Tim) who was the academic wizard, cracked up over his A levels and is passing the time in his father's hardware shop. A few belong to the Cobras, who hang around the Black Hole by day and at night don their gear and ride their Japanese Snakes with the low-slung seats and controls and handlebars on the thin stalk just about the level of their visored helmets.

As for Donny, he's always talking about the contacts he has as if all he had to do was snap his fingers and he'd be a pop star or something. He did work last summer as a runner for some film company but that led nowhere. Most of all, he wants to go to America. That's his dream, his vision. He has posters of Venice, California. He wants Sam to come with him.

The two boys stalk the streets, hunchbacked with cold. At the canal on the edge of town they watch the children sliding and playing. The snow is heaped here, where the fields begin, where they used to play.

Sam dances to warm his feet, tests the snow. It's crunchy, just right.

'Hey! Get off!'

Donny is outraged then forgets his dignity. They throw snowballs, stuff snow down each other's necks, roll in the snow and flop back in it. Two of the smaller girls in Red Riding Hood cloaks regard the big boys rolling in the snow with disdain. The canal is emptying of its sliders and skaters, the oily sun melting.

'You want to go somewhere?'

Sam shrugs. He might as well, though most of the places Donny knows are either deadly or weird. Between the canal and the Black Hole there are the railway sidings and then a kind of landscape of the moon where factories and shops and houses used to be. Life here has rusted away leaving jagged iron so cold it burns, frozen pools, treacherous pits, willow-herb that will flower in the spring, cellars where drifters doss; clues to lives abandoned in a house half-demolished, its face torn off, the revealed privacy of rooms somehow sad, Sam thinks, as if they'd been bombed out and everyone run in terror.

42

Donny squats on a lavatory seat in the middle of nowhere, grunts, gets off, windmills his way to a wall with a door. Knock knock he says, kicks the door open and there's nothing there, on the other side. Sam wishes he hadn't come. The sun's gone. He thinks of being at home with Barney but he's not sure he wants to be there, either. (For quite a long time now he's had this queer feeling that if he goes out he might have nowhere to go back to – as though that creepy house might take off and he'd be left with nothing but his father's pool. He wishes they were still in University Row, though he can hardly remember what it was like living there, except that he felt safe.)

The shells of two terrace houses have somehow survived at the far corner and as Sam stamps his feet and runs to catch up with Donny he thinks, if aliens landed here they'd conclude that a plague or a war had done in a primitive race. (It had started with a fire. A family of Pakistanis had been living there. A woman was burned to death trying to save a child. It might have been an accident but it could have been the landlords after the insurance and the site, Dan says. His firm are after a contract to rebuild, of course, but there's some mystery about the site as if no one wants to build again, though as building land it trebles in value every six months. It's worth so much now no one can afford to build there, so it will probably stay as it is.)

Behind the door there are steps leading up, nowhere, vacant sky above, but Donny jerks his head, come on, and Sam follows him down some unpromising stairs. The snow has driven in here leaving a slippery mush that will freeze. There is a smell of pee. Layers of peeling paint mark the years and here and there some old rosebud wallpaper clings to the plaster. A turn further down still, to the left, and at the bottom a door with a strip of wood fastened diagonally across it. Donny kicks aside a loose brick, picks up a new-looking screwdriver and gets to work on the plank.

'Easy, see. I put in a couple of new screws. Well, what d'you think? Hold on.' The faint light from the grating above gives only the outlines of a largish room. Donny lights a candle stub in a saucer and puts it down on an upturned box. He has developed this irritating habit lately of not being able to stand still. He jigs as if he was tuned into some jerky music you couldn't hear. And cracks his knuckles and snaps his fingers or rolls his eyes. Sort of Rasta stuff.

'See. I got a bed-roll and a paraffin stove. Well, I've got to get a new wick. And cans of food and a saucepan. Just want something to heat them on.'

Sam's gaze is drawn to the far wall. Someone has started a mural. The damp runs down it but you can see it's like something in a child's picture book: giant mushrooms with tiny stick people walking about underneath. A sunflower.

Donny says: 'There's another room through there. Smaller. It's all mine. No one knows about it. A good squat. I might even move in.'

'Move in?'

'Here.'

Donny sits on the bed-roll then jumps up and produces two cans.

'Only Coke. I'll get some beer in later.' He sits down again, his back resting against the wall. Sam sits on the box. He is reminded of the camps they made when they were children. They used to take them very seriously. They pretended to cook grass. The adults were dangerous aliens: very small figures seen from a distance through the branches.

Donny puts down his can and says in an almost ordinary voice: 'It's heavy at home. She's crying all the time. I mean, she looks all bright as if she'd won a prize or something then she starts again. And now he's gone she's on to me. Wants to know where I am, says she'll cook something special then burns it. You don't know how lucky you are. I think she's going mad. Really, certifiably insane.'

Sam listens. He nods. The trouble with Donny is that he talks so much rubbish these days you never know when he means anything. He probably does mean this. At least he doesn't notice if you don't answer, he's so busy inside his own head.

Sam remembers the conversation between Moira and Dan last night. 'My mother's got a nutter. She's going to bring her home.'

44

They are silent for a bit and that is better. Although it's cold, just sitting here, as if you could stay and no one would bother you. Thinking about when they were young, Sam wonders what Lucy would look like now if she were alive. He can't even work out how old she'd be. Ten? Eleven? He remembers bare gums chewing on his finger and a milk smell. Then there is Moira's wild face.

How old is Barney in dog years? His muzzle is grey and his hind legs are stiff.

If you could just close your eyes and stay very still and stop breathing and finish. Not dying like his grandmother. Simply refuse. Go back to that handful of carbon. That's what we're made of. Dead stars.

The light is fading at the grill. The candle won't last much longer.

'I hitched in. I'd better go.'

Outside it's so bitter Sam holds himself tight, trainers slapping on the new snow, which freezes as it falls. Then he begins to run.

FOUR

From the hotel room high above the city Dan looks out at the park. There is darkness there and snow, rimed grass. In the room, as in the Volvo on the motorway, there is no weather. He is happy in the Volvo, always: the almost female way it takes over soothes him, eases his back, swallows the miles so effortlessly there is an illusion that the car is coasting gently while the landscape does the running.

He had arrived regretfully, his back knifing a warning only as he checked in. The receptionist reminded him of Birgit.

'You'll be dining here, Mr Frankland?'

'I don't know yet.'

There was an early Christmas tree in the foyer which recalled, for all its gloss and tinsel and stars, other, deeper woods. That was not long after it happened. After the accident. About the same time he slipped on the apple, just a month later. The Oslo conference on Tomorrow's City. Hot air in a glass-house hotel, everyone wild about the Japanese capsule building, in the same way, through the years, they had worshipped Corb and the high-rise and the terrassenhauser and the domed city and the underwater city.

Dreams of the ideal megalopolis, as if, just out of Eden, you really could start again. Dan, drugged against his pains, had sat it out until in a house high above Oslo he had received grave, courteous Norwegian hospitality and, wandering from the party with a fresh drink in his hand, had found himself in a small room and stood, as he does now, at the dark window, but with a view of a forest, wishing he could weep.

Dan closes the curtains. Now there is no weather. No country even, in this hotel room which might be any in the world. The bottled water for tourists windy of London's recycled urine. For those bold enough to venture into a Europe where if terrorists didn't get you the radioactive air would. In-house television, gift bath-cap, shampoo, bath-foam, well-stocked refrigerator. From which Dan selects two miniature whiskies, adds ice, kicks off his shoes and settles back on the bed. He flicks from one television channel to another. Two soaps, one old Clint Eastwood, Channel Four worrying about the bad news. Dan presses the mute button and tries Radio 3. Beethoven no 6, the Pastoral. Dear old corn, bless it. He closes his eyes but his back hurts, the mattress is too soft.

He thinks of ringing home but that brings to his mind the image of the pool. The small body into which he tried so desperately to pump life, long after there was any point. Moira's stricken face, as if she had been slapped by a giant hand, her unsleeping body rigid in the bed, her head turning away and away.

(That autumn Dan slipped on the apple; the baby, Lucy, had drowned in the summer. No one knew she could walk but somehow she had walked into the pool and drowned at the shallow end.

It was important, they had agreed, to preserve some sense of normality for Sam. Above all, Sam must not suffer. They watched him, hoping he did not notice that they were watching, and he seemed to be taking it as well as could be expected. Of course, he was quiet. When they found he had been playing truant Judith Kraft took him on. Moira seemed to think Judith had done wonders – Sam stopped playing truant anyway – but Dan wasn't so sure. Though Sam really does seem fine now. The dog had been a good idea. But there are moments even now when Dan is aware that Sam spends too much time alone. Or with Barney.

Is Sam too little trouble? Is that the point?)

After all, he does dial home. The telephone rings but there is no answer. Yet someone must be in on a night like

47

this. Probably a fault on the line. The telephone system has been cracking up for years now. Which reminds Dan of the cracks in the foundations of the hospital. The hospital may be sick with concrete cancer and architects can be sued nowadays, like doctors. The University committee is cutting its funding, or, rather, it has not increased its budget, which comes to the same thing. Over-spending a few years ago on in vitro fertilisation: an aspect of medicine that both repels and fascinates Dan who, in a normal, human way, shuns any subject relating to what actually goes on inside his hospital. Moira says he's neurotic about it but he has a horror of the internal workings of the place. Except for the idea (not the sight) of the joining in the laboratory of winning sperm and friendly egg. It should be a cold thought but it amuses, pleases Dan to contemplate that moment when man, like a host at a party, having introduced the two essentials, must stand back and let life decide for itself.

He tries home again. Three heads talking now on BBC 2 but Dan still has the sound muted.

'Moira? Is that you?'

'Bad connection. Dan? You'll have to shout.'

'Where are you?'

'What did you say? What do you mean, where am I?'

Dan can see her, phone wedged between chin and shoulder, trying to light a cigarette. She does cut down but that is a habit she cannot break, as though the ringing telephone threatened her. For a while after the accident she took the phone off the hook after dark unless Sam were out.

'What phone, I mean? Where in the house?'

'The kitchen wall-phone. Why? Sorry, I'll turn off the telly. Hold on. Dan, are you all right?'

'I just wondered. When you pick it up, d'you hear a click? I mean something like a click?'

'Dan, what are you talking about? Are you asking me if our kitchen phone is bugged? Are you drunk?'

Dan eases his shoulder, a shrugging movement. Stretch the muscle, Horseman always says, stretch, hold, relax. Then the dog exercise. When you get out of bed. Even before you walk. Down on all fours. Walk like a dog. Hunch back as high

48

as you can. Hold it. Lower spine. Quadruped walk again. Evolution reversed. Once or twice when Moira had gone to get coffee Barney had slipped into the bedroom. A puppy might have taken this to be a game but Barney was worried by it, faintly disapproving. He stepped forward as though to investigate Dan in dog posture but at the last moment backed nervously. Moira came in with the coffee, her blurred morning sleepwalker's face, her flannel nightgown, the smell of sleep still on her. 'What's the matter with Barney?'

There was nothing the matter with Barney. Nothing at all. There were times Dan felt he could hand over the household to Barney, to his reliability, his grave concern, his fidelity.

'Are you there, Dan? Was the snow bad?'

'A cold coming we had of it, just the worst time of year for a journey, and such a journey.'

'That's Eliot?'

'Yes. No, it wasn't too bad at all. Easy. It's Christmas here already.'

'Yes. Foggertons have done their window. Dan? What was that about bugging? Were you serious?'

'Nothing. Talk about it later. Nothing at all.'

'It could be a bad connection.'

'Yes.' Dan knows that this conversation is pointless but he cannot quite bring himself to ring off. 'Is Sam in?'

'Don't know. He went into town. Just got in myself. It's snowing here. He might be at the Summersons'.'

'He's not driving in the snow?'

'No. I had the estate.'

'As long as he's not driving then. That's all right.'

'He's a good driver anyway.'

(What we don't say, Dan thinks. How studiously we have trained ourselves not to say what we most fear. And never on any account to let him see our fear. The day Sam took off on his first skate-board Moira baked bread. The whole batch sank. I met Birgit on Horseman's couch but I couldn't. Birgit is probably a fairly stupid woman but her flesh had always understood. We drank a little too much whisky. She said: if you're worried about something why don't you ring home? No, she's not stupid. I don't really know what she

49

is at all. I never even asked. The first time it happened my back went in the office and I hobbled across the road to Horseman's without ringing. Horseman had gone but Birgit was there. She was doing accounts. That must have been winter because it was dark at six o'clock. When she apologised that Horseman had gone I asked if I could sit down for a moment and she said, of course. I sat in the black leather chair. I had seen her often before but never really looked at her. Now, watching her do the accounts, I saw that she had an extraordinary quality of stillness: even as she worked her movements were minimal. Her hands were a shade plump, her nails buffed, not varnished. Her upper lip was a little thicker than her lower one. There seemed no need to talk. My back still grumbled but it was peaceful sitting there in that over-heated room.

Birgit squared up a pile of papers and put it to one side.

She said: 'I hadn't realised it was dark outside.'

Then she drew the curtains in both the treatment room and the small office. I imagined there was something wifely about the way she did it, closing the curtains neatly then turning to smile. I imagined all kinds of things about Birgit. At that stage in our relationship everything she did I interpreted as a signal: a meaning in the way she seemed to accept my presence; an invitation? No, my idiot fancies didn't go as far as that. Yet when it did happen I was not surprised. In what we had not said, in the silences, it felt as though there had been a dialogue.

All I knew was that I did not want to go home.

I said: 'I must be keeping you. You should be going home.'

Birgit was tidying the magazines. She put the last one in place and looked at me gravely.

'How is your back now?'

'Not so good.'

'Sitting is worst of all. You'd be better lying down. I still have a few things to do. Why don't you use the couch?'

It was dark in the treatment room. The only light came from the desk lamp in the office-reception room. So Birgit seemed to be coming from the light to join me in the darkness.

I remember I said: 'How? My back.' And she said: 'Don't move. Like this.'

This is all wrong, the way I'm remembering it. It sounds clinical, cold. But it wasn't like that at all. What I felt was an immense gratitude, a letting-go, as if I really were giving her my pain. As if anyone can do that: take away pain. It's difficult enough even to share.)

'Dan? You're not worried about Sam? I said he's not driving. Hold on. Let me sit down.' Moira would be pulling up the kitchen stool closer to the wall-phone, sitting down, her feet resting on the rung. They have a cordless phone but it lives in Dan's office that was once part of the open-plan but now has a door. And a lock. 'Dan, you sound strange. Are you sure you're all right?'

'If there's a power cut there's plenty of fuel in the generator. Moira? Don't forget to turn off the mains first. Is it still snowing? Can you see?'

Moira is amused (irritated?) by Dan's back-up systems. The rest of the world can go into darkness but in Dan's house there will still be light. He installed the generator even before they moved in. He used not to be like this. Before the accident.

'Yes, it's still snowing. More heavily. I can see it in the porch light. It's very beautiful.'

'What? You're fading.'

'Bad line. I'll ring off now. Good night. Sleep tight. Take care.'

'Moira? It's no use. Have to ring off. Can't hear.'

Moira thinks about calling Kate to see if Sam is there but decides against it. She doesn't feel quite up to Kate and Sam is sensible. Although the snow is beautiful, she is still afflicted by snow-tiredness, that odd exhaustion she remembers even from childhood. Something to do with atmospheric pressure perhaps. Dan would know. He's the weather man.

If Sam isn't back by nine, she'll call Kate. She makes a toasted sandwich, pours a glass of wine and carries a tray up

51

one level to the sitting area. It is warm all through the house – Dan's thermostats see to that – but all the same she lights the fire in the hearth for the sweet scent of wood-smoke.

Barney appears. He must have been sleeping on Sam's bed. His coat is warm. He settles judiciously just close enough to the fire to get warm but not too hot.

The red eye of the Sony invites. Bad news time. Moira mutes the sound. Images that through repetition become unreal. A dance-hall blown to bits in Germany. Riot police club down protesters in Eastern Europe. The honeymoon there is over. A wall of fire somewhere in the Middle East. On the African continent the camera lingers with love on a starving child, all eyes, belly swollen with hunger, turning to suckle a dry breast.

Talks about disarmament talks continue. At the time of the Russian thaw, most of the missiles flew away. One base became an American intelligence centre. At another, an MoD chemicals research plant is to be built. For defensive and protective purposes of course. Dan's firm have won the contract for domestic housing and facilities at the new plant.

The firm needs the work badly, this contract will keep it going for a while. Yet when Kate heard about it she screamed at Dan (doubtless, in private, at Howard too). If it is for the MoD, in Kate's opinion, it is suspect. She could be right.

Kate used to go to Greenham Common. She actually took Donny there, slung round her neck in a kangaroo pouch when he was only eight weeks old (was that when Howard began to sleep around?). There was a fervour, a shine about Kate then, she looked like a woman who had a lover. She told Moira, it wasn't at all the way the media portrayed it. They weren't cranks. They were ordinary women like her. The sense of comradeship was amazing. It was the greatest protest women had ever made against the way men ran the world. You see, Moira, women are *for* life. When the airmen bared their bottoms at us it was they who were degraded. Moira nodded. She admired Kate and was vaguely ashamed not to have joined her, but only vaguely. She was writing well at the time and then there was the accident. But perhaps it was more or less than that. There was a certain squeamishness in her, she knew. And a stronger, sometimes life-saving vein of irony. Iron?

(She had been busy enough then saving her own life.)

Moira picks up a book, puts it down. She wraps herself in an afghan and curls deeper into the shabby old armchair that dates back to University Row. It is out of place in Dan's scheme but she won't throw it out. Barney sighs in his sleep and shifts.

It helps to remember that today's bad news is not necessarily tomorrow's history. Dan says he's had it from someone that there are secret talks about an Irish settlement. So the dance-hall is blown to bits but history may yawn and turn over and see these days as a time of hope.

Meanwhile there is Minnie Flynn. A child, who was damaged somehow and cut her wrists. When Moira thinks about Minnie, as she does now, all she sees is the girl with the blank eyes and the starved hair touching a dark window, a strict, black square.

It is at that moment, when she hears the door slam, that Moira knows she has already made up her mind. All this, she thinks, looking round at Dan's room, their habitat rich in back-up systems. We have all this. We are warm enough and strong enough to let in Minnie Flynn.

'Sam?'

Barney's already at the front door. A single wag. He follows Sam up the stairs to the living area. He sniffs at Sam's wet trainers.

'You're soaked. The snow. How is it?'

'It's all right. I kept to the road.'

'I thought you might stay at the Summersons'.'

Sam pulls a face.

'I don't like it there now much.' He doesn't come into the living area but stands on the half-landing that leads up to the bedrooms and down to the kitchen and dining area. He joggles from one foot to the other, perished. Moira isn't fussing about the snow he's brought in. She never makes that kind of drama. Yet whenever he comes into this house

Sam gets the feeling it might be wired for sound or vision or something. Watched. He feels watched.

Moira nods.

'Yes, I know. Poor Kate's not coping too well. It's hard for her.'

Sam shrugs. He doesn't want to talk about Kate Summerson. He enjoyed that run in the dark on the gritted road.

Moira says: 'You'd better go and change. Have you eaten?'

Her son looks so pinched by cold she wants to go over and put her arms around him and draw him to the fire. He has snow on his hair. His face looks flayed to the bone.

He says: 'I'll change and get a sandwich.'

Moira expects to hear the slam of his bedroom door but for once Sam comes back to join her. He squats on the other side of the fire to eat his sandwich. Moira pours wine for them both. He is so cold he drinks the first glass fast and his face flushes. Moira notices that his features are beginning to settle into their final mould. He has her dead father's long jaw and hollow cheeks. Boy's hands still.

She rests her cheek against the high-winged chair and gazes into the fire. Interiors, she thinks. The way things give off signals if you see a room from an unaccustomed angle. Normally she does not pause on the half-landing above the living area but this morning she did and looking down, catching the room unawares, was reminded of a Dutch interior. It was like peering into a van Hoogstraten peepshow box. Dan's black leather sofa, waiting, guarded. The charcoal tweed chair and the orange one Dan brought from Sweden arranged as though to talk. All Dan's things, the paper lantern, the black-stained ash bookcases, the silver eyes of the stereo speakers, disapproving of her old lumpy armchair. And the spaces. The spaces between things were too precise. They threatened. Like the loaded silences in conversations. When they were about seven, she caught Sam and Donny trying to get round the living area without touching the floor. If you touched the floor you were dead.

Moira says: 'We'll have to think of getting a Christmas tree soon. If you want one?'

'I don't mind.' His head is dipped away from her. He has settled on the floor, as close to the fire as he can get, his back turned on the room.

'We've always had one?'

'Yes. Fine.'

'You used to like the tree.'

'Yes.' Sam wishes she wouldn't do this, try to please him and then be hurt because he can't get excited about something she's offering him that is supposed to be a treat. What they never do is to ask him what he really wants. Not that he can blame them for that. He wouldn't know what he wanted if they did ask. When they first got him Barney he didn't want him but now he does.

That first Christmas after the accident there wasn't going to be a tree. Then on Christmas Eve he knew they were up to something. When he was supposed to have gone to sleep he crept out onto the half-landing and there they were below him, decorating this big green tree. The biggest they had ever had. They had even got new stars and proper candles, the sort you have to light. Dan was a bit drunk and she looked ill. Dan turned off the lamps and lit the candles with a taper. It did look beautiful: all those tiny points of light. But something had upset Moira. She turned away. She might have been crying. Dan put a hand on her shoulder but she didn't seem to like that. She shrugged it off. Sam liked the tree but he couldn't understand why his parents were standing like that, apart from each other, as if they were enemies. That is, at the time he didn't think about it. He was too young. But he remembers it now. And how they were the next day: showing him the tree as if they were scared he might not like it.

Now he says: 'D'you remember that year we had real candles?'

'Oh yes!' Moira smiles. She has been unbraiding her plait and her dark brown hair falls to her shoulders. With her hair down, in the kind firelight, she looks younger. 'That was wonderful. How extraordinary you remember. Years ago. I know we were terrified the tree would burst into flames. The first time we lit the candles we turned out the lights.

They were reflected in the window – it was like having two trees. I remember your face. You were so excited. We let you stay up.'

Moira has drawn up her knees under the afghan.

'I wasn't there,' Sam says. 'Not the first time you lit it.'

'Are you sure? I'm certain I remember. How funny.' Let it pass. Don't press him. 'Coffee?'

'I'll get some in a minute.'

Moira has been thinking.

'We might get a tree with roots this year. We could plant it. See if it took.'

Sam nods. He is looking at the fire. She at him. On the floor between them, the dog, the tray with two oranges on a blue saucer. Still life.

Sam yawns. He stands up and breaks the speaking silence.

'Why don't you get a cat?'

'A cat? D'you want a cat?'

'No. I meant for you.'

He is gone and Moira stays on by the fire. She had meant to bring up the subject of Minnie Flynn, to sound out Sam about having the girl soon, perhaps for Christmas.

All sorts of things she meant to say.

She doesn't look but is uncomfortably aware of the uncurtained window. Of course, no one can see in through the black glass. All the same, she has always felt exposed in this house, especially in winter, when she can see out and see nothing but darkness.

Moira thinks of the tree they might get, with roots. She thinks of getting curtains anyway (Dan wouldn't mind. If he noticed). And roots.

She has read somewhere of the Indian banyan tree. Its branches probe the earth with their tips, tunnel, put down roots from which new shoots will grow. Which will in turn support the parent branches. A good principle of nature. Unfortunately, not one that works so well for people. Perhaps once it did. Nowadays our friends are our kin. It is considered all right to resent Mother. No one would be shocked if I put her in a home.

I can't. I couldn't abandon Mother and it is not entirely a

56

matter of responsibility. It is as though we shared a common nervous system. We are connected by my longing and her need. Words that were never spoken are in the air between us.

What I want to know is: what am I waiting for her to say?

Moira rubs the back of her neck. She should go to bed. She hears the click-whirr of the video-tape recorder. Dan must have set it before he left. She flicks on the television to see what he is taping, then remembers there was an Ingmar Bergman film tonight. The film has only just started when it is interrupted by a newsflash. Fifteen pounds of Semtex explosive found in a police raid in north London, along with a large cache of arms and ammunition. Anti-terrorist squad forecasts increased IRA activity on mainland.

Moira turns off the television. The sound of the video-recorder is companionable. She stands up, stretches and walks to the window. The van that she had noticed, parked or abandoned in the lane across the road, seems to have gone. She decides, tomorrow she will look for curtain material. There'll be the party. There'll be Christmas.

The fire is safe to leave. It has died down.

The answering machine. She'd forgotten. Leave it?

A click.

'Moira? This is Judith Kraft. Do you remember we talked about that girl in the hospital? There's rather a problem, I'm afraid. They can't keep her any longer. If you happen to know of anyone? Anyhow. If there's a chance. You might call me.'

Click.

Silence.

London is smiling and shining. Dan leaves the car and walks. Limps, rather. But after the snow the air smells cleaned and he feels invigorated, forgets his back. There is some slush on the roads but in the Park there is still a frosting on the grass. In the old days New York used to give him this sort of charge. Shop windows are dressed for Christmas. Over breakfast he listened to Radio 3 and Vivaldi still sings in his

57

head. But nowadays it is three seasons, not four. Hardly any spring at all except for a day or two. One winter so mild there was a frenzy of speculation about climatic changes. Just as a few years ago the talk was of a new ice age, now the planet is heating up. Or rather, the zones are changing, so England may become as hot as Horseman's treatment room. It is tilting to the East, into the sea. Dan regrets this faintly. He feels himself to be a northern man. He himself is tilting, favouring the left leg.

Lately the beggars have grown more aggressive. They jump out in front of you and shout after you if you don't give. There are daylight muggings. No one who can avoid it travels by tube. And there is a new development – they are bringing their children with them to beg. Old youngsters with skinny, large-eyed infants. On Hungerford Bridge a young man squats with the usual cardboard notice: Homeless. Hungry. He has a small girl with him. The sky has clouded over, a biting wind come up. Everyone is hurrying across the bridge. The boy-father, if that's what he is, looks defeated. It is the child that steps forward and pushes out her hand. A train rattles past, above. Dan empties his pocket of change. He hurries away, stooped before the wind, ashamed.

(She would be eleven now. About the same age as the beggar's child. It is strange how she has grown in his mind. Each birthday he has caught himself looking out for a female child the same age as Lucy. As Lucy would be. There is a children's playground at home, just a walk from his office. Once a year in June Dan goes and sits there. He realises he cuts a strange and possibly suspect figure – a lone man limping towards the bench in a children's playground. One summer the mothers exchanged signals and called their children away. Moira always makes sure she is busy that day. Neither of them speak of it. They would not wish to remind Sam, though Dan has a feeling that Sam probably remembers.)

Too hot now, in the office in the spanking new South Bank block, Dan thinks how much of life is interior. Everyone around this table – three men and two women – is offering

58

a carefully structured image of themselves for the others to accept or to confront.

He has charm. The women particularly are charmed by him.

The chairman is saying coyly: 'Nothing post-Modernist? I fear not a very interesting commission, Mr Frankland.'

Dan is wondering about that click on the phone, the van in the lane, the idea of being followed. What is the word? Surveillance. He is pleased to have thought of it. The windows look out on the bright, wide river. There is rumoured to be a department somewhere. When did people first start talking about the British Gulag? Well, Ireland, of course, but this was nearer home.

'Oh, I'm just a jobbing architect.'

Both women are wearing almost identical pin-striped grey jackets and skirts, white blouses. The younger one however has made concessions. She is sending signals. A clear red lipstick, a vaguely familiar scent, a way she dips her head and looks up to meet Dan's eye. Women are lucky, Dan considers. In their make-up, dress, the way they do their hair, they can decide upon the image they choose to present. Does Moira do that? If so, he is hardly aware of it.

The older woman says: 'Our budget allocation for the habitation units is modest. Comparatively. As you know. But still hearth and home. On the whole we are pleased with the preliminary plans. But the estimate for the fitted kitchens is high?'

'That's the builder's sub-contractor,' Dan says. He knows when to push and when to appear to yield. 'Rising costs. But we'll look into that. I'm sure something can be done.'

She nods. 'Then the gardens. The plots will have to be halved, I'm afraid.'

Dan leans forward. The plans are spread out on the table. He had proposed larger gardens than he knew would be put through, expecting to give up a third. But half?

He explains: 'It would be a great help if you could supply plans for the rest of the site. We need the whole picture to balance one mass against another. Roads, green areas, an outline of laboratories, factories? For instance, here we've

59

indicated trees. A visual screen between the home and work environment. But we've been guessing. We're working in the dark.'

There is a crackle in the room. The older woman glances at the chairman before she speaks.

'The plans of the working units are not available.'

'You mean they haven't been drawn up?'

'I mean they are not in the public sphere.'

Dan's back grumbles.

'I understood this was to be a chemical research installation?'

'That will be its function, more or less.'

Dan knows he is going too far, teasing them. The younger woman is watching him closely. A flick of warning in her eyes?

The chairman puts the tips of his fingers together, forming a steeple. He has the dry-cleaned, curiously sexless air of the higher civil servant who never appears on television.

'Mr Frankland, you will be aware that we put out this commission for tender. Yours was not the lowest estimate. You have also signed the Official Secrets Act.'

'I assumed that was routine for MoD work?'

'Quite. Simply routine.' A thin smile. 'I would ask you not to draw any wild conclusions. Speculation is helpful to nobody.' He is almost coaxing now. 'I am sure we can reach a compromise on estimates. Your firm has an excellent reputation for solid work without flamboyance. No arty tricks. No prima donna temperament. All we ask is that you work within our parameters. And now coffee? And we can get down to specifics.'

Dan nods. In that moment, bleakly, infinitely wearily, he gives in to reasonableness. The firm is small. It needs the contract. Over coffee the climate changes. Everyone is helpful, positively friendly. He gets his gardens.

The younger woman is particularly friendly. Dan doesn't remember what they talk about but his back gradually eases. Sleet slashes across the windows. It will be snowing at home. If there is some secret state, it can hardly be interested in him: a provincial architect of no great reputation, except for one hospital years ago, doing a straightforward housing job, hearths and homes. The young woman has heard of the hospital. She sympathises with his fears for the place.

'So I'm carrying a begging bowl.'

'Good luck.'

Besides, Dan thinks, it's warm in here, cold outside.

He thinks of asking the young woman for lunch but just misses her at the lift.

Outside, he turns up his collar. He is about to set off across Hungerford Bridge when he remembers the beggar and his child. He stands, undecided, then realises he is hungry – a good enough reason for going into the Festival Hall. The musak is Schubert. Daniel gets coffee and a sandwich. There is an elegant artificial tree, white and silver. Hearth and home, Dan thinks, hearth and home. He eats his lunch among Christmas shoppers and drifters and music-lovers and lovers and trippers. The plastic chairs do not give good lumbar support but the music helps. Dan stretches his long frame as far as he can, so pressed-in, and listens to the two cellos talking. After the *String Quintet in C Major* they play the dark *Winterreise* song cycle.

That night on the telephone Moira tells Dan about Minnie Flynn.

'They're chucking her out of the hospital. She has abso-lutely nowhere to go. Would you mind? For Christmas at least.'

'If you want to.'

'I thought we ought to discuss it.'

'No, fine. Go ahead. There's plenty of room. If it won't be too much work for you.'

'I'll get her tomorrow then. How was the meeting?'

Dan remembers the click on the phone, the van in the lane.

'Tell you when I see you. Everything all right?'

'Fine. Drive carefully.'

Dan flops back on the bed. While he is not too keen on this Minnie girl idea, it might be good for Moira. Since the

61

accident she has managed only one children's book and a couple of stories. It strikes him that for the last ten years he has been so busy coping with his own grief he has hardly noticed that the only thing he and Moira ever discuss is whether or not Sam is all right.

It is as though they were standing in separate rooms, speaking to each other. They never talk about Lucy. When it first happened Moira cracked up but since then everyone has admired the way she copes.

Once, when he was rather drunk, Dan confessed to Judith Kraft: We can't comfort each other.

She said: That is quite normal. But you should try.

FIVE

Sam says to himself, Minnie Flynn, Minnie Flynn. Weird name. He is not at all sure he likes the idea of this Minnie Flynn person. He has never heard of anyone called Minnie. He is in his room where he is supposed to be working at the project for next term on the origins of the universe. Of the various theories, he favours the big bang. All that worries him is what came before the big bang. He imagines he must be like those old flat-earthers who could not conceive of the idea of the planet being round.

He can just about get his mind round the idea of the space-time continuum, which he chooses to interpret as everything that has ever happened going on all at once. And if he could crack that, he could snatch his sister back just before she fell into the pool.

Then his parents would not be behaving like secret agents exchanging ciphers. And in his world there would be no Minnie Flynn sitting in the kitchen chewing her nails and looking at him with blank eyes as if he were a worm or something.

Moira had brought her back from the hospital this afternoon along with the Christmas tree. Sam had had to help her heave the tree out of the back of the estate car. The girl had stayed in the car. Then she got out and stood in the slush winding a strand of hair round one finger. She might have stayed there for ever until her feet froze if Moira had not gone back to fetch her.

She brought her in, took her anorak and said 'Let's have some tea,' in a peculiar bright voice. Sam nodded at Minnie but it was Moira he was keeping an eye on. All day, ever since she told him what she was going to do, she'd been too sparky.

When she told Sam, she said: 'You don't mind, do you? It won't be for long and it won't make any difference to you. But I wouldn't do it if you minded?'

'I don't mind.' (He thought to himself, he had suggested a cat, not a person.) 'Have you talked about it to Dan?'

'On the phone after I spoke to Judith Kraft. He says it's fine. She has nowhere to go, you see. Can you imagine?'

Sam thought about that. When Moira had gone to fetch the girl and the tree he had considered the proposition and wondered if it would be so awful, having no home, which must have been what Moira meant. Then he realised that although he wouldn't mind getting out of this creepy house, he always imagined going somewhere. At the end there would be Donny's squat or something like it.

(When he lets his imagination go really wild, or when he can't control it, in dreams, Sam sees Lucy spinning around the earth in orbit for ever and for ever. And no one will let her in.

Most of the time he doesn't think about her because he finds that whenever he does, it is like a door opening on a black hole. It makes him afraid of everyone dying. And now he is older it makes him think of his own death. Sometimes he even pretends he is dead. Once he turned off his light at night, lay very still on his bed, closed his eyes and held his breath. Another time he shut himself in an empty blanket chest, because it was more like a coffin. That was very frightening until Barney came scratching round the chest and whimpering so Sam had to come out.

Sam wonders if he died would they not talk about him, in the same way they don't talk about Lucy. Unless they do talk, between themselves, at night in bed, but he doesn't think so. He doesn't risk talking about Lucy to Moira because he doesn't want to make her ill again, as she was after the accident. Now and then he has thought that Dan wouldn't mind but there has never been the right moment.)

The Minnie person said hello and Sam said hello. And Moira hovered and went on about how they could all dress the tree together, if Min would like that?

'All right,' Minnie said.

64

Minnie looked at her plate. Sam looked at Minnie. Her sweater half-covered her hands so he couldn't see the wrists she was supposed to have cut. When he'd tried out being dead he'd thought of it as the death-game. Minnie must have been playing the death-game seriously. If they ever got to talking he'd ask her about that.

'When you've finished I'll show you your room,' Moira said to Minnie. 'Sam, sometime you could get the tub in for the tree? There's some compost in the garage.'

'There's something I've got to do. Then I'm going to see Granny.'

'You never said? You could have come with me when I went to fetch Minnie?'

'It wasn't visiting hours.'

'Well, fine, yes, she'll be pleased,' Moira said in the kind of voice she used at parties. She told Minnie: 'I can't remember if I told you, my mother's in the hospital.'

Minnie just sat there, arms crossed close to her body, as if she were hugging herself with cold. She had small, grey eyes rather close together. Sam thought she looked like a rabbit, with its ears cut off.

He felt they might all get stuck there. He saw them in the kitchen: Minnie sitting, Moira anxiously hovering, he himself trying to walk out backwards. Then Barney padded into the kitchen, broke the spell.

'That's Barney,' Moira told Minnie.

'Come on, Barney,' Sam said.

'You'll be back for supper? Dan should be home.'

'Right.'

Now Sam lies on his bed, listening to them move about the house. He can hear Moira talking, though not what she says, as she leads Minnie Flynn upstairs and past his door to the room that was Lucy's. It is the spare room now, though they hardly ever have anyone to stay.

Sam hears Moira go to the towel cupboard, then she calls out: 'Anything else you need,' and goes downstairs.

The one good thing about Dan's open-plan is that it makes this a great house for listening. When Sam was young he used to leave his door a crack open and pretend he was an alien receiving messages from Urth: the only blue planet in the Universe. Sometimes the messages were good. Urth-She would be cooking and talking to the early form of life which must just have emerged from the soup of creation because it did not have proper Urth words. Or Urth-He would be playing his music. Mozart climbed the stairs, paused on the half-landing, slipped round the door.

The wise alien considered the signals from this planet and judged them to be good. Until something happened and Urth fell silent except for whispers and the telephone talking to itself, unanswered, and when She was alone an awful noise like someone choking to death.

Then the alien left and Sam was on his own. Except for Barney, who arrived about then or a little later.

Sam gets up, stretches and has a look in the mirror. He scratches his chin. If he's going to see his grandmother he'll have to shave. Perhaps he'll go tomorrow. On the other hand, he likes his grandmother and feels sorry for her. It must be awful being old and no one wanting to look after you. Whenever Moira talks about her, her voice goes tight. He knows she doesn't like going to see her.

But it's dark now and by the time he got to the hospital it would be almost the end of visiting hours.

Sam looks again at his project laid out on the desk surface, built in when Dan planned this house. He takes his A4 pad, felt pen and the first half-page he has written back to the bed. He elbows Barney to the other side of the bed and props himself up with a pillow to read. The beginnings of life. The origins of man. It's part of the humanities curriculum now but he did all that stuff ages ago in primary school. He remembers the headings: 'What the Bible says' and 'What the Scientist says'. But most clearly, suddenly he sees the picture he was so proud of at the time, of the Garden of Eden. He was allowed to bring it home and Moira kept it for ages because she said it reminded her of University Row, with the deep green lushness and the wobbly sunflowers. Sam ponders. Perhaps she was right. Perhaps the garden from which he first saw the world was a kind of paradise. Or

66

that was how it seemed to him. Before the accident. He doesn't much like talking about that time. It embarrasses him to think that there was a time when he expected only good things to happen.

'Anything you want,' Moira says. She knows she must resist the inclination to fuss and yet she is reluctant to leave Minnie alone.

'It's a small room, I know, but it faces south.'

Minnie is sitting on the edge of the bed just as she was when Moira first saw her in the hospital. All the way home in the car she said nothing, just chewed her nails and made Moira feel she herself was chattering idiotically. Moira has enough social assurance to deal with anyone but she has never met anyone quite like this. So she concentrated on the driving – once off the main road the ruts of mud and snow had frozen – and reviewed in her head the fantasies she vaguely entertained of, in some undefined way, 'saving' Minnie.

She had imagined that she had got some response, however minimal, from the girl the last time they met, and envisaged building on this, very carefully, very tactfully. From what Judith Kraft said, she guessed that direct questions would get her nowhere. The only way to play it was to treat Minnie with ordinary friendliness and hope that she would open up. In her fantasy Moira saw Minnie as a nervous animal gradually drawing security from the three of them and their relationships with each other – even taking her place to square the circle.

The trouble was that ordinary friendliness felt so artificial and sounded so noisy. She must talk to Dan about this.

The tree, for instance, had seemed a good idea. Almost a symbol. Moira had decided before she set out that on the way back she would take Minnie to buy the tree. She saw them making a ceremony of the choosing of the tree, a ritual such as Sam had always enjoyed so much when he was small. The farm they used to go to a quarter of a mile from their own house had become a garden centre. A good one. They even had trees with roots. Moira saw herself explaining to Minnie that they must find the tallest and the most spreading, even telling her as they picked their way among the trees, how this used to be a family ritual.

What actually happened was that Minnie didn't even leave the car. She waited while Moira chose the first tree that seemed remotely suitable, queued inside, paid with her credit card and with some difficulty got a bored assistant to help carry it back to the estate car.

It was so cold by then the low sky might have frozen over. Moira blew on her chilled hands. On the way back to the house she turned on the radio. They were playing a Christmas carol. She drove rather carelessly, too fast, considering the state of the track. As they neared the drive up to the house she nearly skidded as there was a thump on the windscreen and something too large and dark fell away. Images again, she thought, and shivered. Her hands were actually shaking when they pulled up outside the house. There was blood on the windscreen. A crow, she guessed, poor bird.

Then Minnie said: 'I like that smell.'

For a crazy second Moira thought she meant the blood. Then she realised the girl was talking about the Christmas tree.

Now she looks at Minnie sitting on the edge of the bed and accepts wryly that Sam has not fallen in with her master-plan to make Minnie feel part of the family. After tea he made the first excuse he could to dodge off.

'There's a portable telly somewhere,' Moira says. 'I'll find it as soon as I can. The radiator's on. It's thermostatic. I mean it adjusts itself according to the temperature. So you don't have to bother with it. Come down when you like. We'll eat about eight. Daniel might be back then. That's my husband. Shall I pull the curtains?'

'If you like. I don't mind the dark.'

'That's funny. I don't like it.'

For the first time Minnie responds. That is, she raises her head and speaks directly to Moira.

'You must be scared of something.'

'Well. Maybe I am.' For Moira the dialogue has taken an unexpected turn. She straightens a towel on the rail by the basin and wonders if this whole Minnie business is not the most appalling mistake. 'Min. You don't have to stay here, you know. It's only if you want to.'

'I know.'

'Fine. Well then.'

Moira leaves the room and goes to the towel cupboard. She gets out the big grey bath-sheet Dan will want if he showers when he gets back. There is a magic, a comfort in such things: counting the warm-smelling towels, seeing herself for a second as the good woman in a folk-story whose house is always entirely in order.

Moira calls to Minnie: 'Anything you need', leaves the towel in the bathroom and goes downstairs. The idea comes into her head of writing a children's story about this good woman. As she gets the supper – peeling potatoes, chopping onions – Moira tells herself this story she might write: of the good woman who lives in a cottage on the edge of a forest. Her husband is probably a wood-cutter. Every morning he eats his porridge and goes off into the forest. While he is away the good woman sings as she works, keeping house. She fetches water from the well. She washes the porridge bowls, which are white, with a blue flower motif. She smiles at her baby in the crib that her husband made himself, decorating it beautifully with carvings of birds, flowers and squirrels. He has set it on rockers so perfectly cut and balanced, just the touch of a toe from the good woman as she works will set it rocking.

Moira looks doubtfully at the chicken joints. Have they really defrosted? She takes a gulp of cooking wine and sets them browning in oil. Could it be the ghost of a housekeeping person inside her (the person Moira imagines her mother was hoping for)?

Turning the joints with a spatula, Moira sees the good woman sweeping her floor with a broom, while on her stove in a black pot a marrow-bone simmers along with fresh vegetables from her garden. A marmalade cat snores by the stove.

The woman is so good she does not know that she is good, simply that she is happy with her orderly house: the

69

smiling dishes ranged on the polished dresser, the snoring cat, the singing kettle. She hums as she looks out on her sunny garden where, as by magic, there bloom all at once flowers from every season. She will go outside in a moment to cut some flowers.

God, I hate this woman, Moira thinks. She empties her glass, fills it again and pours the rest of the wine over the dubious chicken. I would like to blow cigarette smoke in her face. I would like to do something witchy to her. Make a gingerbread doll and stick pins in it.

Turn down the casserole, put on the lid.

The forest is deep. The husband could be eaten by a wolf?

Soft-hearted Kate would not like that. When she read to Donny all those years ago, when she reads to Poppy, she looks for stories with endings to send them happily to sleep. She censors the wolf.

Ha! Got it!

First the leaves rustle (remember the forest is very close). Then the flower-heads are wrenched from their stalks. The good woman's washing is snatched from the line. Round and round it whirls as a door slams shut, a window implodes, the sun goes in, the sky is dark and a devil wind, all the way from Mesopotamia, sends down a furious spiral and sucks up into the vacuum which is its centre flowers, cottage, good woman, every one of her housewife spells. There they are, spinning up and round and up – marmalade cat, wholesome stew, blue and white dishes. The good woman's skirts and petticoats fly up, and she reaches but fails to catch the crib as it tumbles over and the baby falls out. When the bough breaks/The cradle will fall/Down will come baby/Cradle and all.

But it wasn't a breaking bough or a wind from Mesopotamia. It was an accident.

Moira gasps and sits down heavily. This is how it always hits her. She can never predict when some ordinary train of thought will lead her treacherously to that sharp pain. These occasions are not like the crack-up. Then she had turned to stone in Foggertons' household linen department

70

(and what the hell was I doing in the linen department?).
All she remembered about that was knowing she couldn't
move or breathe. And someone asking if they could help.
Faces, anxious and curious. Everything too bright. Voices
muffled, coming from a great distance, even Dan's. They
had got hold of Dan somehow (did they look in her bag,
find her credit card and someone perhaps knew the name?)
and there he was. The man she knew to be her husband,
behaving like a husband, loving, concerned, frightened. Even
the stone woman could see that. And yet at the hospital
when they said he'd have to leave, the stone woman felt
nothing but relief. She had no responses for this person,
her husband.

But winded by pain though Moira is, this is not like the
crack-up. She knows how to handle it. She sits in the kitchen
chair and breathes as in labour: lightly, on the surface, then
puff, a big breath out. Breathe, puff again and the kitchen
ceases to whirl, she puts her face in her hands then draws
her hands away, raises her head and knows that she must
get on quickly with something else. Movement, action, are
essential.

Get salad bowl, rub with garlic. Judith Kraft said, 'If you
want to talk. About anything.' Not just Mother – anything.
I do. But I can't. Won't? Olive oil, tarragon vinegar, where's
the mustard? What I feel is beyond the healer's touch, beyond
healing. Ever. Never. Never to be free of. Wooden spoon,
just enough iceberg lettuce in crisper. I lead a busy life, an
ordinary life. My disablement is not apparent. Shred lettuce.
It bleeds a rosy, slightly milky liquid. At first, when friends
searched my eyes, they looked for mad Demeter, feared the
failure of crops. But when the stone woman breathed again
she learned to contain her grief. Her rage is house-trained,
dry-eyed.

Put plates in warming drawer. Its red eye watches me.

For months after it happened there were letters from Eleusis.
Every other woman, it seemed, had lost a Persephone. Dan
intercepted the mail. There was one woman who rang and
rang, a cracked voice from chaos. I wouldn't answer the
phone. We went ex-directory.

71

It was a year before I could make love. Then Dan had the big hospital contract and he worked all hours. He slept with someone, I'm sure. I didn't challenge him. It seemed important to preserve an appearance of normality, for Sam's sake.

Where's Dan? Could be tricky driving on the motorway. Turn on the radio for the weather.

It was Sam playing truant from school that shocked me awake. Judith Kraft was so good with him. Wanted to ask what he said, she said, but knew I shouldn't.

Good. That's over until the next time. The radio says there are delays on the motorway but only one accident, no fatalities.

The further I get from the stone woman, the smaller she grows. A matter of perspective. Dear Kate credits me with courage. It's not that. It's a matter of putting one foot in front of the other, deciding you are strong enough to take in Minnie Flynn. (This winter's mad images come from another country where the stone woman lives.)

Damn. Ought to ring Kate. The hospital for Mother. Save Minnie Flynn. Stop smoking. Get my hair done. Lose weight. Make list for party. Make list for Christmas. (Kate and I have often said if women stopped making lists the world would come to an end. We made a pact once not to write a single list for a week. But a week wasn't long enough. They just raided the freezer.)

The radio is saying something about attempts to sabotage the Irish talks. The IRA are believed to have possession of Libyan rocket-launchers funded by Noraid. It has gone on so long that one almost stops hearing. No. One hears and sees but stops feeling.

The conifer propped against the wall is giving out its scent like a blessing. Moira still has faith in the power of the tree: a vision of the three (no, four) of them around the tree, its arms spread in a magical benediction.

Moira switches to Radio 3, sinks back in the rocking chair, shuts her eyes and for that moment both irony and sorrow are suspended, as the music twines with the good cooking smell and the sharp-sweet pine.

72

And Lucy is there, like a flying child in a Chagall, older now, three or four. In her nightgown she is a white wax candle, an angel, a daughter free in space, laughing.

As always, just as Lucy is about to speak Moira wakes. Sam has come down. He is saying something. The dream has gone.

On the motorway Dan sees the lights flashing ahead. An accident. It has not been bad going so far. When he arrives single-lane traffic has just started moving again. He joins the queue and passes the accident. An ambulance man is tending a figure sprawled on the ground. A little blood on the snow. A woman, probably in shock, sits on the hard shoulder, wrapped in a red blanket, her face in her hands.

Dan turns up the radio. The *Haffner* has reached the point in the first movement where the triumphant happiness of this domestic symphony dips for a moment into sadness. Dan knows to wait and Mozart will come bounding back, clowning, singing.

As he drives on, cautiously, the darkness folding its wings behind him, Dan realises that he is not looking forward to Christmas. Moira's Christmas. Since the accident neither of them has had any heart for Christmas but they have done it for Sam. The crackle of Christmas paper makes him wince. He usually drinks too much at their Christmas Eve party. He tries to remember how the party ritual started, whose idea it was. Anyway, having started, they seem unable to give it up. He sees it now as a noise they make to block out some mysterious unspoken argument that is always on the verge of breaking out at this time of year.

In the past few years Dan has managed to slip off at some point to meet Birgit, in Horseman's surgery or his own office. He'll miss that, though not as much as he imagined.

What would have happened, he wonders, if he'd gone to lunch with the girl from the meeting and they had spent the afternoon in bed? Sex helped but not that much, he

73

had learned. By now he'd have the Mozart melancholies, he guessed. 'What's the matter?' she'd have said and he would have answered: 'Nothing.' And he would have been thinking of Lucy and perhaps he would have said something about the beggar and his child. Or asked if she knew anything about surveillance, the click on the phone, the van in the lane.

For years after the accident, by some unspoken complicity Dan and Moira gave Sam absurdly extravagant presents. He unwrapped them and played with them then after a week or so they would disappear into the toy cupboard. Sam played with the presents in a curiously sober way.

As if he were watching them watching him.

Dan gets home at midnight. Moira has been reading in bed. Her spectacles have slipped down her nose. She is wearing an old cardigan over her flannel nightgown and her hair fans out all around her. The book has fallen from her hand and she only wakes up when Dan gently takes off her spectacles.

'Supper? There's plenty left.'

'No. Bed.' Dan is undressing. 'I had a sandwich at one of those Disneyland pull-ins.'

She smells whisky on his breath.

'Was it awful? How's your back?'

'Fine.'

'And the contract?'

'You know. Give a little, take a little. Usual compromise. Smaller kitchens, larger gardens. Settled anyway. If Howard agrees.'

They lie side by side. Moira snaps off the light.

Dan had thought he would go to sleep at once but he can't switch off the mood of driving on the dodgy motorway. After all, his back does twinge.

'How's your waif?'

'Waif? Oh, Minnie. You know she's Irish?'

'No.'

'Well, you can hardly tell. She doesn't talk much yet. Barney seems nervous of her.'

'Sam?'

'He's not talking, either. Dan?'

'Yes?'

'It's silly. I've got her and I don't know what to do with her. I suppose Christmas will help. I got the tree.'

'Mnn.'

'Are you asleep?'

'No.'

'Some bird smashed itself on the windscreen. Rather a mess, I'm afraid. But it's a beautiful tree. I thought we might get real candles again. Well, it doesn't matter. Your back does hurt, doesn't it? Here. Move over.'

Her touch is not Birgit's but it helps. Dan begins to relax. He'll sleep soon. Moira rests her face against his back. This is one of the times they could have made love.

Dan sleeps. Moira wonders: do men dream about their children? She kisses his back between the shoulder blades. She resolves: we'll make this a good Christmas.

Sam is watching *The Brother from Another Planet* about the black man pursued by slave-owning extra-terrestrials. He likes the Brother and his clawed feet. It's a good film. The only thing wrong is the happy ending. They'd never have run away like that, once they'd got him cornered. They'd have sent for reinforcements and made slaves of the whole earth.

His father's come in so he supposes he can go to sleep.

At supper the Minnie Flynn person wasn't so bad. She didn't eat much or talk but she didn't expect him to talk, either. And if she changed the way she looked just a bit she wouldn't be so depressing. The only thing really awkward about supper had been the way his mother seemed to be expecting something to happen, like everyone being happy suddenly.

Minnie checks out her room. She looks under the bed, opens the cupboard, smells the soap by the wash-basin.

She is by no means sure she'll stay here but she'll give it

a try. It's a nice room. For a minute she is puzzled by the transfers on the walls of birds and clouds and rabbits and bears, and the tiny chair in the corner.

It's like walking into some crazy fairy story. Then she understands. This was a nursery. A baby lived here.

SIX

Christmas is coming. Indubitably. It cannot be held off. The Franklands will have their party. They always do. It is the best party of the season. Like the labour of childbirth Moira forgets until it comes upon her what hell it is.

'Summer's so much easier,' she says, wondering about making canapés or getting them from Foggertons' deli. 'I can't think why we don't do it then.'

She looks at her lists and knows quite well why they don't have a summer party. At the last one they had the accident happened.

All through the preparations for the party and for Christmas – the cooking, the ordering, the telephoning, the shopping, the wrapping – Moira has been visited by unasked-for, unwelcome memories, pangs of nostalgia and of pain so vivid they make her dizzy.

Partly it is Kate. She rings or has to be rung or seen every day. So just as Moira has her coat on to go into town to buy presents (whatever can she get for Minnie?) the telephone rings and it's Kate. As Christmas approaches her river of tears is swelling to an ocean. Like a child who believes in Santa Claus she cannot believe that the wandering Howard will not be magically returned to her. (What does she expect, Moira thinks, to find him gift-wrapped on the doorstep delivered by Red Star?)

Moira looks at the telephone, nearly doesn't answer. As she grows older she finds that compassion takes an enormous amount of energy. She has almost given up lame dogs (what about Minnie?). But Kate is Kate. They have shared so much of life, so many years, the good and the bad, Kate has won rights.

So Moira leans against the wall, one finger hooked through her car keys and glances through her list as she listens to Kate.

Today she sounds tremulous but at least she's trying.

'Moira? You sound funny. Are you standing up?'

'No.' Moira sits down on the kitchen stool.

'Did Dan get back safely?'

Mother: plant. Dan: tape? Kate: smoked salmon, and champagne to weep into. Sam??

'Yes. No problem.' Neither eaten by wolves nor stolen by trolls. Moira fumbles in her bag for a cigarette. Britain has the highest rate for death by breast cancer in the world: a statistic she finds hard to credit. Someone's cooked the books. Books. *The Snow Queen* was always her favourite winter story but Sam never liked it. Fairy stories seem to be much on her mind at the moment for reasons she cannot fathom. A couple of months ago a feminist publishing house offered Moira a commission to do over popular fairy tales, reversing the traditional sexual roles. The working title was to be *The Sleeping Prince*. Moira was flattered but found the idea too absurd to contemplate. She told Kate who said, yes, but she didn't see what was so funny about it.

Now Kate is coming to the point.

'Moira, have you seen Howard?'

What Kate means is, has Moira seen Howard's girl. Yes, Moira has. She has never understood what girls saw in Howard. So skinny and bony, that wisp of pale beard, balding. She is fond of Howard but sees him as a gerbil. His girls are usually his students. He works for two thirds of the week as Dan's partner, one third as a lecturer. He always seems to choose the same type: clones of Kate, thinner, less interesting, twenty years younger.

Kate doesn't wait for the reply but comes to the point of the call.

'I can't stand the thought of Christmas this year.' Tears are very close now. 'All the time I'm doing things, getting presents for Donny and Poppy, everything, I keep thinking

78

how it used to be. You know, when the children were small and we filled stockings and Dan dressed up as Father Christmas, all those things.' Here comes the flood. 'Moira, do you remember?'

'Oh yes, I remember.'

If only I could cry like Kate. If only I could cry. All I could manage were those terrible heaving gasps. Kate cries for dead birds, Ethiopian children, Howard's infidelities, she cries so easily and then her face is clear, washed like a sky after rain. Kate cried for Lucy so that as we embraced it seemed that I was comforting her.

'Moira? Are you still there?'

'Yes.'

As suddenly as she started, Kate has stopped crying. The weather at the other end of the telephone has changed. The sun has come out. Moira can see Kate standing, smiling, in a pool of tears.

'I meant to tell you,' Kate says. 'It's so funny. There's a couple moved in down the Row. And she's got *fifty* of everything! Can you believe it?'

'Fifty of what?' Moira says. Sounds like my good woman who was sucked up by the tornado, she thinks.

'Everything! Loo paper rolls, bars of soap, cans of soup, dried curries, tins of condensed milk, fruit, meat, aqua libra, tuna, dog-meat.'

'What for? A fall-out shelter?'

'No. Not specifically. Just a sort of bolt-hole.'

Moira smiles. 'Dan would die of envy. Maybe that's what I ought to give him for Christmas. You are coming to the party? I haven't asked Howard.'

'Well, in that case, yes. If you're sure?'

'Of course I'm sure.'

'Wouldn't it be simpler if neither of us came? I mean, it's always been the four of us.'

Cloud over the sun. Precipitation imminent, Moira guesses.

'Sorry, love, got to go. Shopping.'

'Oh, Moira, I forgot to ask how it's going with the girl?'

Moira reaches for her scarf from the peg by the door.

'Well, it's not really going yet. Too soon.'

'I'm so stupid! She's there, isn't she?'

'Yes. Bye then.'

Moira checks that Minnie doesn't want to come into town. The girl stands on the half-landing and Moira wonders how long she has been there. For a mad second she hesitates to leave Minnie alone in the house (all those knives). Sam's already out. It is absurd the way she is tiptoeing around Minnie, not asking, somehow propitiating, as though the girl were a dangerous presence in the house. Christmas. Christmas must help.

Driving into town, Moira reflects: it could not have been as good as we remember in University Row. The snow-plough has buried the hedgerows under snow so that all around the landscape is white. It could be a white Christmas. In the days Kate weeps for we were simply young and nothing bad had happened to any of us, nothing of any seriousness. So, looking back, we see ourselves framed in a summer garland under a giant sunflower like the one in the painting Sam brought back from school. There we are. Kate's fatter, I'm thinner, then one of us will be lying in the hammock cradling a pregnancy. And there is music and I am thinking of the fairy tale I am writing and will get published. The children play safely and we are returned to our own childhoods, vicariously, through our children. (Freda, my mother, kneeling, tending her flowers, wearing a straw hat tied under the chin, she was very beautiful, I must have been the most terrible disappointment.) And the men will come home soon, on Saturdays there'll be a barbecue, but meanwhile the women are complete in themselves, in each other's company, in a way the men cannot imagine. And Lucy who will have one Christmas, her first and her last, waits to be conceived, has not even entered this world.

We were so happy.

Or were we just smiling for the camera?

Donny wags his head in disbelief.

'It's true,' Sam says. 'She hardly eats at the table but she's pinching food.'

80

Kate is out with Poppy so they are sprawled in Donny's room in the house in University Row.

When he was young, Sam thinks, he used to envy Donny this attic room. He has a ladder he can pull up behind him. He still envies him that but is no longer so enchanted by the chaos. Not that he's tidy himself but all this stuff is too much.

Donny was first given this room when he was eight. Before that they'd thought he might forget about the ladder and fall through the hole. So it's like radio-carbon dating. Everything Donny has owned from the age of eight is in this room. When you walk anywhere you crunch underfoot the broken plastic toys. There are: laser guns, Daleks, those robots from *Star Wars*, a Scalextric racing track, Lego, and some things so demolished they can't be identified. There are: a Teddy bear with one ear and one eye, several heaps of comics and movie magazines, a dart-board, a spaceman's helmet, a hamster cage (empty) and a cross-bow. Sam remembers it all, to some degree it is his past too, but he remembers the cross-bow best because they got into trouble about it.

From the dormer-window let into the attic they had tried to shoot a sparrow in a tree at the bottom of the garden and nearly killed Donny's grandfather who was asleep in a deckchair under the tree. He died quite soon after but that had nothing to do with the cross-bow. At the time Donny said the old man had got like a baby and had to be taken to the lavatory and everything so it was good he died. That was around the time of the accident, about a year after, when Sam had been playing truant but before the death games. He remembers thinking about death, though. He couldn't imagine his own at that point, he was much too young. But Donny's grandfather dying made him look at his parents and wonder how soon they would be old.

Sam flops out on a bust bean-bag. With the window shut and sealed for winter this room smells of Donny's socks and Donny, who is very close to having a BO problem. Sex is supposed to put that right. Donny claims he had it with an

81

extra when he was a runner on a film but Sam suspects he's lying. He's still got acne, a fairly revolting case. Well, not exactly lying. Donny's so stuck in his fantasies he probably believes them himself.

When Donny is doing his fantasies and being really irritating, cracking his knuckles and twitching and yattering about the good grass he smoked last night, Sam wonders why he's his best friend (practically his only friend). Then he realises it's because he has known him always, since they were both as young as Lucy was when she died, so he's probably stuck with him for ever.

It's like looking down the wrong end of a telescope, remembering how it was when they all lived here in University Row. One Christmas Dan dressed up as Santa Claus. Sam pretended not to recognise him but he knew. Then in summer he sees himself and Donny and the others playing in the gardens. It's a freeze-frame in which they appear as small as extra-terrestrial pygmies in a high forest of bean-rows and flowers.

Mouser has followed them up the loft-ladder. She doesn't like the smell of Barney on Sam but she trusts him more than she does Donny, who pulls her tail and rubs her fur the wrong way.

So she has settled on Sam's chest, pinning him down while he tries to explain about Minnie Flynn.

'I've seen her take the bread. She stuffs it in her sweater. That's all she nicks – bread.'

Donny grunts. 'Well, you said she was a nutter. She's probably an axe-murderer. What's she like?'

'Irish.'

'Hey! You know that joke about three Irishmen changing a light bulb?' Donny has been jiggling a bald tennis ball. Now he throws it at the dart-board. 'I was thinking. I might go and work for *New Musical Express*.'

'The point is, my mother's got Minnie for something. But I don't know what.'

Sam looks at the poster of Venice, California. Seems all right. Blue sky, sun, a board-walk, white wall. But he doesn't believe Donny will ever get there. He doubts if

82

he'll even leave this house to go and live in his secret pad on the waste ground. The furthest he'll get is the Black Hole, until everyone has gone away and there's no pack to lead.

Not that he's any better than Donny. He has almost made up his mind now to leave school. He thinks just as much about sex, which on one level of his mind is all the time. Last summer, he nearly did it with Sally when she was one of the pack before she went to work, but now he tries to picture her face, he can't. It's funny about girls who were at school with him and in the Black Hole pack, girls he's known most of his life. He can imagine having sex with them in ten years' time but not now. They're too much like sisters.

After having sex, Sam's fantasy is to own nothing, never to be possessed by things in the way everyone seems to be in the end. Like Christmas. Moira's making a terrific business of presents this year, more than usual.

Suddenly, Sam feels very sad when he thinks he might grow out of Donny. That is, they might meet somewhere in a few years and have nothing to say to each other because one had changed and the other hadn't.

'What d'you think will happen to us?' Sam says.

Donny scratches his chin.

'Nothing, probably. Because we'll become an uninhabitable planet. You know, cows' farts and stuff destroying the ozone layer.' Donny sounds awed. 'Just think of it. All those cows farting!'

'I've got to go. Said I'd see my grandmother. Get off, Mouser.'

'Why don't you bring her to the Black Hole? That girl, I mean.'

'I might.'

Donny has put a tape into his ghetto blaster. The Beatles are old men now but they're back. Sam hovers, his neck cricked under the attic roof. From here he can see the tree where Donny's grandfather was sleeping. He wouldn't mind dying under a tree.

Donny is listening in exaggerated ecstasy.

83

'*Lucy in the Sky with Diamonds*,' he says. 'You know that meant LSD. Everyone was doing it then. Out of their skulls.'

'Yeah. Right.'

Whenever he hears this tape Sam sees Lucy. Up in the night sky there, and all the stars are diamonds. It is not a sad thought or a happy one. Just a picture in his head.

Driving past the hospital, Moira sees Sam, hunched in his anorak, loping up the drive between the conifers. (The trees had been an enchanting feature of Dan's first model, set down in a scene like a child's play-set. Here's the church and here's the people. There's the spire and there's the steeple. Or was it the other way round? In any case, the last, long, record-breaking summer has burned some of the beautiful, green-feathery trees to death. They are yellowed now and will not awake.)

Moira sees Sam but Sam does not see her.

The hospital. Dan's statement. Years and years ago, Moira remembers, Dan and Howard, all the architects they knew, were building a brave new world of tower blocks. Higher and higher they rose with the fervour of medieval masons. There was a passion to those days. As it turned out, a mistaken crusade.

She sees Dan sitting a little apart from the rest, less engaged, as though he knew already how it would all end. Sitting sideways on to the big pine table, his head cocked in a characteristic gesture, eyes bright, faint smile, over his high cheekbones, watching. Wistful too, like the wise child who wants to join the party but knows it will end in tears.

Even in those days was Dan already expecting the worst? Even before the accident?

That evening they all have supper together: Moira and Dan and Sam and Minnie.

Moira had intentions for this supper but somehow the day has stolen all the good-woman spells in her bag. Full it was when she set out, but somewhere on the way bony little fingers have interfered.

84

She serves the chicken (overdone), passes round the salad and baked potatoes (underdone). This is the wrong sort of kitchen. The light is too bright. The absence of interior doors threatens. How could Minnie – hunched as usual, skinny wings folded, pushing the food round her plate – possibly feel at home here? But then, where would she feel at home? What else are they supposed to do? The girl can't be anorexic, Judith Kraft would have told her. Dan has tanked up in his study on just enough whisky and Mozart, he's talking to Minnie but getting nowhere, of course. If anything, his presence has driven the girl deeper into silence.

Dan is saying: 'Where do you come from in Ireland, Min?'

From Minnie's expression when she raises her face to answer him he might just as well have slapped her.

'Country.'

Dan can see that's all he'll get. He glances wistfully at the television but does not turn it on. Sam is eating but not talking.

Moira refills her glass and Dan's (Minnie has not touched the wine) and decides not to try with Minnie. Like a cat or a dog or a child, it may be the best tactic to ignore her until and if she decides to join in.

So behave normally.

'How was Granny, Sam?'

'She doesn't like it there. She wants to come out.'

'Well, yes, she would. I mean, I wish she could.' The hell with it. Moira speaks across the table to Dan.

'I've been thinking I might do those stories after all.'

'Stories?' Dan blinks.

'You know, the role reversal ones. *The Sleeping Prince.* Only that's Rattigan, isn't it? The Old Man who lived in the Shoe – that sort of thing.' A pleasing spark of malice. Moira grins. 'Could be fun. One-parent family cracks up. Only this time father gets the blame.'

'I thought that kind of feminism was old hat?'

'Lines are drawn up. Final battle still to fight. I suppose that'll be when men get compulsory womb-implants.' Moira reaches for a cigarette, lights it. She's drunk enough Tesco's plonk to give up for the moment the Happy Families act. If Min wants a surrogate mother she can take her as she is. Her bones ache with trying.

Dan says: 'When I was a child I was always scared of fairy tales.'

'You're supposed to be. It's the way children face their deepest fears. Death of a protector. Abandonment. Sex.'

'So I suppose I didn't want to.'

'Face your fears? Probably not.'

Sam, and Min from under her hair, are watching the dialogue across the table like spectators at Wimbledon.

'Well. Pudding,' Moira says. 'I meant to make one but this is Foggertons' blackcurrant cheesecake. Or cheese or fruit. Min?'

Min shakes her head then she takes an apple but does not eat it. She holds it tight, all the same, like a squirrel with a nut. Not that she's so pathetic, thinks Moira. Herself in witchy mood, she catches a glint in Min's eyes, puts a pointed hat upon her head and sends her whizzing round the room on a broomstick.

For a blink, the kitchen tilts very slightly. Dan is saying something about a new burglar alarm system. Moira steadies herself, closes the fridge door and puts down the cheese. It's not the wine. Snow nerves? A message from the stone woman? All right now. Sitting down. Talking to Dan about the party list.

They agree. The usual people. Dan has turned on the television but with the sound off.

Moira says: 'I asked Kate. She'll be so lonely.'

Sam tunes in to Dan. Danger in the air.

'But I've asked Howard. Kate's got the children.'

'And Howard's got his girl.'

'But we've always had Howard.'

'We always have Kate.'

Dan is bad at initiatives. She's the one who conducts the weather in this house.

'Well,' she says, 'we can't unask them. They'll just have to work it out.'

All the same, Moira thinks, she should warn Kate.

There will be no confrontation. War will not break out today.

But what Sam wants to know is, who are they acting for?

Sam is watching *2010*, an old video cassette he got in a sale, when he hears Minnie Flynn coming out of the bathroom. She pauses at his door and he says: 'Want to watch?'

She shrugs and comes in. Barney stiffens. He is still courteously cautious of Min.

'Nearly finished,' Sam says. He indicates a bean bag and Minnie Flynn sits down. She folds her arms across her chest and pulls up her knees to her chin. Her hair hangs down. He can't see her face. She looks as if she might get up and bolt, any minute. That's fine, if that's what she wants to do.

'Seen it before?' Sam asks.

Minnie nods. 'And the other. The first one.'

There's the monolith again, the one with which the first film opens.

'What d'you think that black thing is?'

'I think it's a coffin,' Min says. Her tone is matter-of-fact. The film ends and she gets up and walks round Sam's room, still hugging herself, her fingers bunched inside the frayed cuffs of her ratty sweater. Sam has looked in the cupboard where Moira keeps Christmas presents, wrapped and unwrapped, just checking up (he has always felt since he was small that he ought to know what is going on in this house, he does not like surprises). He guessed that the big soft blue sweater with the reindeer pattern was intended for Min and wonders now if she'll ever put it on. He can't imagine her in it. It's too rich.

Min is behaving like a cat at the moment, inspecting new territory. She glances without interest at his creation – project papers, posters, video cassettes, then stops in front of his postcard peg-board.

'I like pictures,' she says. She is looking at the Max Ernst of the Moon in a Bottle. 'That's under the water, isn't it?

87

The moon looks frightened. And you can see people and a fish. There's a little girl. I like the colours.'

'You can have it, if you like.'

'Oh no,' she says. 'No.' And turns into herself again, closed up.

At the door she turns.

'Was there a baby in my room?'

'Yes. My sister. She drowned.'

'That's terrible then.'

'It's all right now. It was a long time ago.'

When Min has gone Sam settles back on his bed, but he isn't ready to go to sleep yet. Three scientists are talking about the greenhouse effect. One has a moon-head, the other two narrow heads like fish. Moon-head frowns. He says this sharp winter is an aberration. The greenhouse effect will reach catastrophe level in one decade not three. The first to go will be the eastern and southern coasts.

Boring. Sam changes channels. Three more heads are discussing chemical warfare. It sounds a pretty horrible way to go. By comparison, one head says, a nuclear strike is clean, provided, of course, that there are no survivors.

Sam switches off. Although he has given up the death games he realises he thinks a lot about death. Or rather, about his own dying: bang, slam, black door. Donny expects to live for ever and that's probably normal.

It might partly be his grandmother. She was making jokes about how horrible hospital was and asking about him. She always seems to have time to listen (his parents start out listening. They used to listen. But nowadays he can see when they stop listening and start pretending, so he's more or less given up trying. At other times Moira seems too anxious to listen and then he can't think of anything to say. That is how it has been for a long time.) Today, although his grandmother was pulling a face at the ward sister's back, Sam could see there was something different about her. She looked smaller and somehow scared. Perhaps she could see the black door. He wanted to ask her but he wouldn't, of course.

But she is old and that's different.

88

Sam looks at the ceiling. If it's got to come he likes that idea of a clean strike because although he hasn't thought what happens beyond the black door (the monolith) he'd rather other people went with him, just in case.

Lucy had to go alone.

Moira is repentant. The full moon stares at her. Dan always sleeps with the curtains open. When he is away Moira pulls them. Dan turns onto his right side, his back to her, when he feels ready to sleep. They have two mattresses on the king-size bed: one hard for Dan's back.

Moira says: 'We'll dress the tree tomorrow.'

She is thinking, I am allowing Min to get on my nerves. I am handling the whole thing badly. Even if I had offered Min motherliness I should not expect daughterliness in return. I have simply offered her a temporary haven. If she wishes to she will respond, answer questions, in her own time.

Anyhow, what do I know of daughterliness? Father died too long ago to be anything more than a benign, tired presence. I was old enough to know he was dying, too young to accept it. So I put away feeling. Freda came down the beach, shading her eyes against the light, wearing a crisp cotton dress, to tell me he was dead. I sat on the beach. I turned my back on Freda and picked up pebbles. One by one I flung the stones of grief into the sea.

And I can guess what Freda thinks of my daughterliness, my hefty, ungiving presence. A certain voice I use with her and no one else.

Dan says: 'Forgot to tell you, I've got to go to London again. I'll try and get back. Summons from the Ministry.'

But the tree. You must be here for the tree.

'Isn't it Howard's turn?'

'Howard irritates clients. He's so used to having his own way in the lecture hall he tells them what they ought to want. Anyway, he's got flu.'

You mean he's got a girl.

'You'll be back for the party?'

'Oh yes. Wouldn't miss it for the world.'

89

Dan turns his back on her. He is sleeping or pretending to sleep.

Moira wonders what happens to a marriage. There is a man and a woman. They are alone together. Then one morning they wake up and find they can hardly see each other, they are signalling, at best, across all that is gathered to a marriage: children, responsibilities, saucepans piled high, needs, furnishings even. East of Eden, Adam and Eve mourned Abel, fretted about Cain and went shopping for kitchen units.

Well, we're all right, Dan and I.

The moon keeps Moira awake. Reading doesn't help. She takes off her spectacles, turns off the light and lies down. To help herself drop off she tells herself a story, a device she has used ever since she was a child. The story she tells herself is of a woman who lives on the edge of a forest. (She is not the good woman. She is neither good nor bad.) Every day her daughter wants to play in the garden and every day the mother tells her: 'Yes, you may play in the garden but you must never go into the forest.'

She knows her daughter is a good child but all the same, children are children. So every so often as she goes about her cooking and her cleaning and her weaving, the woman calls to the daughter, playing among the sunflowers and runner beans: 'Daughter, daughter, are you still in the garden there?' And the daughter answers: 'Yes, Mother, I am here.'

Then one day when the woman is sweeping the floor she pauses to call to her beautiful daughter, with the blonde plait, hair the colour of snow over which a lemon sun has melted: 'Daughter, daughter, are you still in the garden there?' And the daughter does not answer, even when the woman calls again and runs into the garden calling.

When she cannot find her beautiful daughter in the woodshed or between the rows of runner beans or in the dog-kennel or down the well, the woman does not pause to think or to take off her pinafore or to call the dog, but runs straight into the forest.

In she plunges, forgetting even to do as her husband used to say and pick up a handful of white pebbles to mark her way. Deep, deep she runs. Brambles snatch at her. Fallen branches trip her. And as she runs she calls: 'Daughter, daughter, are you there?' The old forest answers with a creak, the breeze with a sigh. Squirrels watch, birds chatter of the mad woman running in the forest but never the daughter answers.

A day and a night and a day have passed. The woman is weak. She picks berries to eat and kneels to drink from a stream. At night she smells wolves gathering behind her but at dawn she runs on again.

She has not wept until now but at last in the deepest heart of the forest where day is nearly as dark as night she calls for the last time and, covering her face with her pinafore, weeps bitter tears.

Then a twig cracks, leaves rustle and the answer comes: 'Mother, Mother, I am here!'

The woman is so happy she forgets to scold. The daughter too dries her own tears, for she had lost her way and wanted so much to be by her home hearth with her mother.

So the woman and the daughter embrace and talk and kiss all afternoon.

'Oh, Mother,' sighs the daughter. 'I followed a bird and then a squirrel and then a deer. And then I was altogether lost and frightened of wolves. Now take me home.'

'Hush, hush,' says the mother, cradling the daughter who rests with her head in the woman's lap.

She strokes her hair, the colour of snow over which a lemon sun has melted, and is so happy to have found her that hours pass and dusk falls.

Only then does the woman realise that neither of them may ever see home and hearth again. For in running after her daughter she had forgotten to pick up a handful of white pebbles to mark her way. So although they have found each other in the deep heart of the forest, both are altogether lost.

The daughter sleeps, dreaming of hearth and home.

91

Her mother waits for the coming of the wolves. Already she can smell them. Soon she will see their yellow eyes all around, slits in the night that let in their dreadful fire. She sings to her daughter and when the girl opens her eyes, smiles and whispers: 'Sleep, daughter, sleep.'

In her room Min adds the apple to the hoard of scraps she keeps in a plastic bag under her bed. Some of the bread is going mouldy already.

She sits on the edge of her bed and rocks herself. She daren't lie down yet, not until she is too tired to sit up, for when she closes her eyes it always comes: that knocking on the door, then she opens the door and the first of the men says sweetly: 'Does Johnny Flynn live here?'

SEVEN

*I*t is a morning of brilliant hoar-frost beauty. Dan leaves early to drive to London. Moira wakes charged with energy. Days like this when the earth and trees are white and the wind does not blow and the sun shines are one's childhood returned. She knows this to be a temporary grace, no absolution, but her head sings with stories as she cleans the house. The tree is in peat in a bucket, waiting to be dressed – Moira dug out the old decorations yesterday and bought real candles.

(On a day like this she is wearing a red bobble hat, about to make her first solo ride on her sledge. Her father waits at the bottom of the white slope, and she knows he will catch her.)

Today Moira does not mind this house. The normally threatening emptinesses, the silences between Dan's strict furniture, hold the light that pours in through the yards of window. Through the window she sees Sam and Min sliding on the bottom of the pool. Ice has turned it to a skating rink. Barney can't get down the slippery steps. He patrols the edge of the pool, half-anxious, half-excited. At first only Sam slides. Min stands hunched at the shallow end wearing an old anorak of Dan's. The sleeves are too long. Her hands have entirely disappeared (and her slashed wrists). She watches, then with uncertain steps joins Sam, wobbles, nearly falls, he catches her. With sliding steps they make their way to the deep end. They pause there. They seem to be talking. Well, Min talks to someone, thank God. Sam glances up, scans the windows, but it's the glass you can't see into, only out of. Moira wonders about the apple core and the mouldy bread in a plastic bag

93

she found when she pushed the vacuum-cleaner extension under Min's bed.

Moira left it there. Perhaps she will talk to Judith Kraft about it. Meanwhile she wants to keep this day at least, intact. She wants to put a spell upon it (if the frost cracks the tiles in Dan's pool, so much the better: we can do without that pool). She puts away the vacuum-cleaner, makes coffee, sits at the kitchen table, sees the greenness of the apple on the pure white dish and hears the radio talk about blizzards to the north and south. (Will Dan be all right?) And now in the studio we have a discussion on child sex abuse. After the news. Coming up shortly.

Off. The gales blow outside all our lives. The most one can hope for is a warm bivouac in a windy world. On one of those winds Min blew in (and Lucy out). Yet a bivouac can be a world in itself, complete, enough.

I shall write my fairy tales but they will not be feminist nor happy nor unhappy. I shall spin my own world according to the queer darting images that come to me, some of which make me smile. They may be sharp. The story-teller may have a wicked beak. But I shall not let in the stone woman. I shall use my magic and forget that which should be forgotten. No one will publish but I shall write. And then say Amen.

Sam trudges back to the shallow end, his sodden trainers cracking the ice. He wishes Moira hadn't sent Minnie Flynn out of doors with him. She's depressing, with her ratty hair hanging down. He can't stop thinking about the mouldy bread but he can't say anything because he shouldn't have been snooping in her room in the first place.

Anyway, he's supposed to feel sorry for her and in a way, he does. And he seems to be the only person she'll talk to. Now she's asking questions in a sort of hungry way and the peculiar thing is, Sam doesn't mind answering, or not as much as he would have thought he might. And perhaps if he answers he can ask her about death-games, if it was a game or if she was truly trying to kill herself when she slashed her wrists.

Min says: 'Did your sister drown in here?'

'Yes.'

94

'D'you remember it?'

'Just. I was only seven.'

'Is that why your parents are so unhappy?'

'Are they? I suppose they are. Not unhappy exactly. But they never talk about Lucy. They always call it the accident. I think that's stupid. It makes Lucy more dead. As if she hadn't been alive at all.'

Sam doesn't really want to talk about any of this. He doesn't know why he's said what he said.

Dead leaves have been trapped under the ice. One of the blue tiles is cracked. Dan will be upset: his precious pool. Sometimes Sam thinks his father is the loneliest of all of them. He knows what goes on in Dan's study. He pretends to be working, turns up the music and drinks. He never talks about Lucy but now and then Sam has had the feeling that Dan would like to say something, when they've been together, just the two of them.

If someone could be blamed for what happened to Lucy it might be easier for everyone.

'OK, Barney, I'm coming.'

Sam climbs out of the pool. He doesn't look back to see if Min is following. He hugs the dog, then gives a great 'Yip!' and the two race, shaking the icing from the trees until Sam trips and Barney barks, plants his front paws on Sam's chest and the boy and the dog roll down the lawn.

Min squelches into the kitchen. Moira thinks, at least she's got some colour now, if only on the end of her nose. Oh, my God, I forgot to give her boots.

'Min. Hang up your coat and take off your shoes. I've got some mules somewhere. Here. And coffee. I've just made it.' (Are you a waif or a witch? Do you belong to stories or to life? And what is the difference, anyway? Stories have a beginning, a middle and an end. People don't. Not a middle, anyway. Is it something cracked in me that seized you, to bring back on a north wind and set a gale blowing in this house? To spit in my good-woman stew? Is it that I want to break something so I bring in a wrecker?)

'Black or white?'

'Don't mind.'

95

Moira puts in milk and sugar. On second thoughts, more sugar. The poor child's hands are blue with cold.

'You must be – ' Moira starts to say when the telephone rings. She is conscious of Min, her hands cradling her mug for warmth, watching.

'Howard. What a surprise. How are you?' Why don't you get your hair cut? It was fine when we were young but now there's nothing on top, do you really imagine those greasy, greying locks are attractive? And that wispy beard? Well, apparently they are. To Kate and the younger female. 'Did you want Dan? He's in London. But you must know that.'

'It's you I want, Moira love. The party. You know. Is it OK if I bring Sheila?'

Sheila? Oh, of course, the proto-Kate, twenty years younger.

Moira keeps her tone judicious, she hopes.

'I don't think that would be a very good idea.'

'You sound queer, Moira. Is there someone there?'

'Yes. All I mean is, Kate's coming.'

'Ah.'

'Dan didn't tell you?'

'Not actually.'

'If you'd rather not come?'

'Wouldn't miss it. Never do. Does Kate know I'm coming?'

'I'm going to tell her.'

'Well. We're all grown-up after all, aren't we?'

Moira shrugs.

'More or less.'

'Right, love. Fair enough. See you then. OK?'

'Goodbye, Howard.'

Moira hangs up the telephone. Min has disappeared. Gone upstairs. She has left a dirty coffee mug and a puddle of water just inside the back door.

With Christmas only three days away, London is in a foul mood. The snow falls thinly and turns at once to slush. People walk hunched, thrusting, heads down. Pavements and roads are clogged. In the concourse at Liverpool Street,

96

Dan struggles to elbow his way through the crowd. A woman whacks him on the face with a parcel. Pointless to try for a taxi. Christ our Lord is born today, sings out above them all. A red-robed figure – Santa on his way to work – kicks Dan's ankle. His Achilles' tendon screams. The tube journey which should take fifteen minutes comes out at closer to an hour. There are several inexplicable stops in tunnels between stations and as Dan makes his way to the surface at Waterloo he sees that those coming down are attempting to reverse their passage, milling like frantic souls at the mouth of hell. The speaker squawks urgently. The turnstiles going down are locked. Two vaguely official figures are struggling to control the confusion as those who would go down meet those coming up.

When he finally breaks out Dan sees the hastily scrawled notice in wonky capitals: UNDERGROUND CLOSED.

After all, he'll only be fifteen minutes late. After the tube the air seems almost fresh, the whip of cold wind welcome. He pulls up his collar and jams down the old seal-skin hat, a survivor from the days of brutal innocence. The pain in his ankle has settled down to a quiet grumble. He strides out and sees there are fresh graffiti on the hoarding opposite the station. The spray-paint messages have lately become more aggressive. One JESUS LIVES. A couple of UP YOURS MATE. GOD FUCKS. Then a more enigmatic statement that even Dan in his haste finds intriguing: TREACHERY AND TREASON ARE THE HEART'S TRUE REASON – JUDGE AH WEY. They cleared Cardboard City a while ago but it sprang up again and has continued to do so every time it is demolished.

Inside the new Ministry building with its self-contained air, deep carpet and business-like security desk, Dan feels himself to be an interloper: a weary, limping figure who brings in the weather with him. As he waits to be cleared he looks up at the TV monitors. I am a watchbird watching you.

In the halls of the Establishment it seems they do themselves proud. The architectural style is vaguely Pharaonic. Ramses II would have been proud of the bombastic bronze surrounds to the wall of lifts, guarded each side by open

papyrus capitals – post-modernist quotes at their most gran-
diloquent. And they haven't stinted on the marble either. The
Christmas tree is hi-tech steel hung with polished ferrous
icicles.

The security men have the double-glazed eyes of customs
officers: they see your heart but their souls shine not forth.

Dan presents his letter, explains himself, wonders what
would happen if, instead of waiting for them to consult their
check-list and make their telephone calls he were to bolt for
the lifts. He imagines he might get three yards at the most.
One of the security men bends to speak to another sitting
at the desk and Dan notices a serious-looking bulge under
his jacket on the right side. He must be left-handed.

'Thank you, Mr Frankland. If you don't mind.'

Now he is being frisked. Someone slipped up last time.
Dan thinks of the van in the lane, the click on the phone.
He opens his brief-case for inspection, closes it again and
accepts the clip-on identity disk: VISITOR. To be surrendered
upon leaving the building.

'If you will wait there, you will be met.'

The impulse to make a nervous joke in the face of dangerous officialdom.

No.

But the whole thing, the entire set-up (or what Dan
imagines to be a set-up) from the van in the lane to this
pantomime is one murderous, paranoid conspiracy. In the
lift with the male secretary to the committee, Dan eases his
back against the mirrored wall of the lift, closes his eyes
for a weary second and opens them again to see that he
goes on for ever, that he is surrounded by himself, his
own reflection given back again and again, repeating and
diminishing and repeating. Mirrors are the way in to the
underworld. He who goes through becomes a *shaman*. He
may return to the bright spring but he will be dead, though
there will be those to swear they have touched him and he
lives still.

All done by mirrors. Tricks. Reflection and refraction give
me back more images of myself than I can bear.

'Sorry? Yes. Shocking weather.'

'The Chairman apologises. I'm afraid it's just me. It was only a detail anyway.'

It is the younger of the women from the last meeting. Clare something. Today she is wearing a soft high-necked grey dress. When Dan came in she was standing at the far end of the conference table, her back to the white light. She comes forward to meet him. 'I am sorry. We shouldn't have brought you up for this.'

'I'm sorry I'm late.'

'You weren't on the tube?'

'Yes. There was some sort of hold-up.'

'You didn't know? There's been a bomb at Oxford Circus. I mean the underground. We haven't heard much yet but it seems to be bad. Please, won't you take your coat off? I've sent for coffee.'

Dressed like this she seems very slim, less assured. The secretary has left them. Dan's plans are laid out on the table.

'You see, Mr Frankland – '

'Dan. Please.'

'In that case, Clare. Clare Fowler.'

Dan nods. 'So what's the problem?'

'No problem really. It's simply that on your revised elevation – here, see – you indicate a children's play area there.'

'That was agreed early on, surely?'

'Yes. But not the siting. You'll have to move it, I'm afraid.'

'Why?'

The slightest hesitation.

'It's in the security zone, you see.'

Dan pushes his hand through his hair.

'And what's in the security zone?'

'Nothing. That's the point. A sort of cordon sanitaire.'

Dan sits down heavily. He remembers when this contract first came up, Kate Summerson screaming at him: murderer. But poor Kate would have said that about any MoD job.

'Perhaps you could explain. Is this cordon to keep people out or in?'

A longer hesitation this time. She looks at him as though

99

hazarding his reaction before she decides to answer: 'Both. That is, primarily the first. The second only in the most drastic situation. Which is unlikely to occur. But we have to envisage every scenario. If you understand.'

'I'm not sure I want to.'

'No.' With the light on her face she looks strained. She shakes her head as though to say, not here, not now. Or to deny something.

'No problem,' Dan says. 'We'll resite it.'

He decides to walk to the Strand. With the snow falling and the tube closed there is little chance of a taxi but it might be worth a try. Or that is how he rationalises his impulse to cross the river by Hungerford Bridge. Only when he fails to find the beggar and his child does Dan acknowledge to himself that he was looking for them. There are beggars and children but not the young man and not the girl.

Just as he is standing, feeling foolish, uncertain what to do next, a train rattles past above and someone catches his sleeve.

Clare is wearing a grey cloak.

'Are you crossing the bridge?'

'Yes.' Dan nods. Ask her for a pub lunch, you fool. You want to and you know exactly what will happen if you do. Tell her all about your limp, your loss. The comfort of women. Tell her you're looking for a dead child.

But she seems to have some purpose. It is even possible that she has waited for him to get out through security and followed him. She stands for a moment beside him, looking down at the river. She is wearing grey gloves.

She says: 'I like the snow, don't you?' And in the same conversational tone of voice: 'You probably guessed. It's not defensive research. They're going to manufacture nerve gas. Organophosphorus. A sort of human insecticide. Please forget I told you this. I'm chucking in the job but I'd prefer to go my own way.'

Then she is walking away from him briskly. Not so fragile after all. And Dan stands stupidly under the falling snow. He is alone on the bridge with the beggars. Someone is playing *Silent Night* on a mouth-organ. Then there is the thin voice of

100

a home-made flute. A river-bus scuttles below. In the snow, among the beggars, Dan pulls out his wallet from the inside pocket of his heavy jacket and empties it of notes. Most are snatched at once. A couple are carried away and drift calmly down with the snowflakes to settle and melt and dissolve on the urgent tide.

Moira has been counting on the tree and, as it turns out, there is some magic.

She started that afternoon, half-heartedly, by herself. Sam had helped her carry the tree to the living area, close to the window, then he had gone out for a run. Min had gone upstairs after a lunch she had not eaten. Moira counted the fruit when she put it out and checked it afterwards. No one had eaten a banana but there was one missing. Gone to join the mouldy bread.

At first Moira thought she would keep the decoration spare: simply the real candles and the tree. Then as she began to unpack the decorations from the egg boxes, she found herself remembering, and as she remembered she dressed the tree.

Like household gods, she recognised the silver tinsel stars from University Row, the golden pineapples from the flat in Camden Town the first year she and Dan had lived together. They had agreed, no room for a tree, then both brought home covertly, to surprise the other, the same small artificial tree. They had put them on tables, one each side of the gas fire. The trees had been lost long ago or thrown out in one of the moves but the pineapples survived and with them, as she hung them among all that sweet scent, there came a wrenching memory of the secret first Christmas of all, when they had taken the phone off the hook and locked the door. They were complete in themselves then, with no thought of what lay buried in the future: the accumulation of debris and needs (and loss) that a marriage collects, like a drag-net trawled across the sea-bed.

'That's nice.'

Moira was sitting on her heels, her long skirt spread around

101

her, when Min, coming downstairs silently, made her jump. Moira smiled.

'Yes, it is, isn't it.'

(What is it about the child? She brings the weather with her. She comes from the land of the stone woman and the chill is still upon her.)

The tree is like a warm camp-fire, Min a feral animal, circling before she dare close in.

'Can I do some?'

'Of course. I'd be glad.'

Moira stood, easing her back. They worked together, Min slowly, but surprisingly she stuck at it.

'Oh, look,' Moira said, 'this angel. Bit battered, poor thing. I remember it when I was a child. Did you have a tree? I mean, when you were small?' (Ask no questions, you'll be told no lies.)

'Oh, yes.' They were working in near-dark now but Moira was reluctant to turn on the light. 'Yes,' Min said, 'we always had a beautiful big tree.' Moira could not see her face, just her pale fingers at work. They looked like the tentacles of some submarine creature. 'We'd plant it after Christmas and dig it up next year. I lived in the country, you see.'

'What country? I mean, where?'

'Oh, just the country. I liked it there. We had fields and flowers and a white house with blue shutters. And a swing. I remember the swing. And I had a pony and a cat and a dog.'

Moira kept her tone even, casual.

'I suppose you could go back. To Ireland, I mean.'

'Oh, I couldn't go back.'

'No? Well, why don't you put the angel just there, at the top? Then I'll light the candles. Or you can, if you like.'

It is a pity Dan isn't there but this will do. Sam is back from his run just in time. Barney barks. Moira hears the kitchen door shut.

'Sam? We're just going to light the candles. Bring up the wine. And three glasses.'

So that is how Dan finds the three of them — his wife,

102

his son and the cuckoo's child, all in the dark around the lighted tree.

Minnie Flynn sits in front of her bedroom mirror. She won't go to the party but all the same she has put on the clothes Moira lent her. She doesn't like them much, though if she'd nicked them that would be different. Things you've taken are all right. When she had the house to herself she went right through every room. She didn't take much. Just a small blue ring from the bottom of the woman's jewellery box, two plain white handkerchiefs, some pills from the bathroom cabinet, a toothbrush that hadn't been used and a tiny pair of gold sewing scissors. It wasn't so much the things as the feeling she got taking them and knowing that she had them. She hid them inside a press-on sanitary towel and put it back in the box. The sewing scissors were a bit dangerous but that was part of taking things, being scared in case you're caught.

It was nicking a car that got Johnny into trouble and brought the men to the door but Minnie doesn't want to think about that. It was that thinking that got her in the hospital with people asking all those questions. She said she'd forgotten and that was true, she had forgotten most of it. And if you forgot hard enough, you were free to be someone else. You could be a girl who lived in the country and had a pony. Then the other Min would be dead, who opened the door and it was dark and raining and they took Johnny away.

Min thinks the clothes make her look like a diddicoy but she is interested in the make-up. She puts on the face stuff, foundation and powder in one, first in dabs then thick, so her mouth and her eyebrows disappear and she can paint them in any way she likes. There is a pink lipstick and a purple one. She goes for the purple. It is the colour of blood and Min grins at herself in the mirror: a vampire, that's what you are, Min Flynn.

Her reflection makes Min feel different, powerful, as though from the mirror she had summoned someone else, a person you'd have to watch out for.

103

The mirror person is displeased with Min's hair: so lank and mousey and thin. The Woman and everyone else are busy with the party downstairs. Min nips into the bathroom and finds what she is looking for. They are not proper scissors for the job but they'll do. Min grabs at a fall of hair and begins to cut.

EIGHT

Everyone comes in from the cold, offering cold cheeks to kiss, stamping the new snow off their boots under the porch-light, handing their coats to Sam to hang up.

They say what they say every year: 'Sam! Haven't you grown! Hasn't Sam grown, Moira?'

'Well, actually,' Moira says, 'we think he's stopped.'

Everyone looks at Sam. He smiles and feels the colour rise in his cheeks. He is thankful for the blast of cold air to cool down his face, though it will be playing hell with Dan's thermostats. (Dan is getting the drinks, helping himself along the way. Sam has noticed, since the last trip to London there has been something peculiar about Dan. He seems distracted. After work and after supper he goes straight to his study and drinks. Not that he gets drunk. No one outside the family would have any idea, Sam judges. He guesses it is either some problem to do with work, or else an affair. When Sam told him about the cracked tile in the pool he just nodded.)

Once Sam has taken most of the coats he can go upstairs. Or maybe he'll have to help carry round the eats. Minnie Flynn was going to do that. Moira found her a skirt that came almost to the ground and took in the waist. She gave her a blouse and a quilted black sleeveless jacket, and some make-up as well. But Minnie hasn't come down.

After all, it can't be more than fifteen people. Perhaps the snow and the winter bug going round have kept some at home. Until Moira herds them into the living area there is a danger that they might be spread too thinly in the open-plan.

105

Even so, some escape into Dan's study, where they have set up a bar.

'Come to the fire,' she says.

'Lovely tree.'

'Real candles.'

'Yes. Excuse me.' Someone else is arriving and Sam has ducked upstairs. Min has not come down. Everyone seems to have heard about Moira's waif and wants to see her. It will be just as well if Min doesn't appear. Moira has changed twice: from red to black and back again. The black made her look ill. The red is somehow an over-statement but it used to be Dan's favourite: an ankle-length jersey dress with a scoop neck. She wears jet with it and heaps up her hair. Just where she pushed in the last pin there is a knot of tension in her scalp. That odd sensation that things are tilting around her has returned. Not that she will fall but that the big bad wolf will come and blow her house down. (Dan's house, not mine. Never was.)

Moira moves through her party against the flow. In the half hour she allowed for changing once everything was ready, she looked at the Valium in the bathroom cupboard but did not take it. Only three left and anyhow it makes her thirsty. Instead she had a shot of straight whisky, pulling a face at the taste. Then she brushed her teeth twice so there lingers in her mouth the flavour of mint and malt mixed.

'Kate.'

I forgot to warn her, Moira thinks. Oh, well, with the weather and the bug maybe Howard won't come. Too late now, anyway.

'Hope you don't mind, love.'

'No, of course not. Let me take something.'

Kate is standing on the doorstep. She is wearing a fringed shawl over her best black, with a large and heavy-looking bag on one shoulder and Poppy on the other.

'Oh, God, I'm sorry. You don't mind, do you? The sitter's got the bug and you know Donny. I mean, you can't rely on him. I've brought Poppy's toys and blanket and things, if I can just tuck her in somewhere, honestly, she'll be no trouble. I can't tell you, it's so wonderful to get out.'

106

'For heaven's sake, Kate, come in. Let me shut the door. And Poppy's five. She can walk.'

Kate holds the child to her like a shield against the world. Against all danger, reality.

'Oh, but she's asleep, you see, and she had this cough. After the rash. I told you about the rash?' A figure appears behind Kate. 'And Donny's been parking the car. That's all right, isn't it? I mean, he can be with Sam?'

'Yes. Come on in, Donny. You'll find Sam somewhere.' Moira knows what Kate is up to. She is only surprised that she hasn't brought the washing machine and Mouser. She wonders if she should tell her that Howard is coming but decides against it. He is probably in bed with the Sheila thing, recapturing the vigour of his youth.

'Can I put Poppy in the spare room?'

At last, Moira has got both Kate and Donny inside and shut the door.

'No, Min's in there. It'll have to be our room.'

'Oh, of course, your waif!'

'I wouldn't describe her quite like that.'

The bell rings. Sam has disappeared, upstairs presumably. Over there Dan has been captured by two of the younger University wives. He is wearing his listening face, head slightly to one side, eyes down. A nod then he throws back his head. A burst of laughter. One of the women has her hand on his sleeve. Moira attempts to signal. Dan's eye is not to be caught. The bell rings again.

Kate is saying: 'I think you're so marvellous doing this. The party thing.'

'I think I'm off my head. Why don't you take Poppy upstairs?'

'Bless you. I do hope she doesn't wet the bed. It's since Howard went. It's her way of saying that she feels guilty, poor darling.'

'Yes. Well. Must answer the door, Katie. Hurry up and tell Dan what you want to drink.'

Someone has answered the door. There is a gust of cold air. The wicked witch of the West, Moira thinks, wonkily, out there in her wellies, waiting. There is actually snow on the indoor mat. Dan's thermostats will have a breakdown. The house of glass will implode.

She takes a good gulp of her red wine and when she looks up again there appears to have been some kind of parthenogenesis. The party has increased itself. There must now be well over thirty people and they have begun to break away from the living area and spill down the stairs, onto the stairs, into the study. Moira thinks, there is a musical analogy somewhere. The prelude is done, the conductor has flung down his baton and if there is a plainsong beneath, it is muted. Counterpoint has taken over, everyone singing their own song with their hands over their ears. That is to be expected, it is the mark of a good party.

There are a number of faces Moira cannot remember ever having seen before. Dan's secretary Isobel, who is in love with Dan, who hasn't noticed the fact (though Moira has), has brought a new boyfriend. She is talking to him animatedly, all the time scanning the party over his shoulder for Dan. It must be interesting in that office, what with the lovestruck Isobel and Howard the Pouncing Gerbil. And Dan off somewhere else in his head.

Moira has given up the idea of passing round the nuts and olives. Foggertons' canapés (dry stuffed eggs and cardboard sausage rolls) have pretty well gone. There are more in the kitchen. First though, Moira knows she should circulate, carrying the last full dish.

The doorbell rings. The telephone rings, both at her elbow and in Dan's study, which Dan has abandoned, leaving people to help themselves to red, white, the Widow and orange juice. The Veuve – twenty bottles – was delivered yesterday: a handout from a construction engineer Dan has sworn never to use again. There was also some very good claret from an Australian pirate developer who wants that waste site on the edge of town and thinks Dan has influence with the planners (he doesn't).

Moira covers one ear.

'Hello.'

It is a female voice.

'Hello. Sorry, you'll have to speak up. Terribly noisy this end.'

'Can I speak to Daniel Frankland?'

'There's a party going on. I can hardly hear. Could you call back? Tomorrow?'

'It is rather urgent.'

'If you give me your name? Hello, are you still there?'

Someone has opened the door. There are Judith and Morris Kraft.

'I'll ring tomorrow.'

'Can you leave your name?'

'Fowler. But it doesn't matter. I'll call.'

Moira puts down the receiver and pulls out the plug. Fowler. What could be urgent between Dan and a female called Fowler?

'Judith! Morris. Have you left your coats? Lovely to see you.'

'And you are lovely to see, Moira, my dear.' Morris beams. Nice man. (A still from summer: Morris sitting at the shallow end of the new pool. A woolly mat of hair on his chest. They have all drunk a little too much to celebrate the pool. Judith is floating, her hair fanned out, still young hair, a rich chestnut. There is music. Dan has put on *The Magic Flute* and turned up the amplifiers. Careful. Watch it. That first remembrance will lead inexorably to the other.) Judith's hair is grey-streaked now but she is a good-looking woman still. A woman, it strikes Moira, who is in possession of herself. Friends can be divided between the grown-ups and the children. Kate is a child. Judith is grown up.

'Come and get a drink. D'you know everyone? Dan's around somewhere. Ah – over there.'

Dan is standing near the tree, his back to the party, looking out of the black window. The perfect host.

'A real tree and candles!'

'Yes, I'll light them in a minute. You'll be all right? I must get some more eats.'

'Shall I light them for you?'

'Oh, Morris, would you? There's the taper. Thank you.'

Moira makes her way through the crush down the steps

109

that demarcate the living area. On the lower level are Dan's study, her desk and the front door. (It is here that Sam put up his wigwam years ago, soon after they moved. Moira remembers Dan down on his knees trying to reason with Sam.) Elbows stab her, backs part only reluctantly to let her through. No one seems to have noticed that the candles have been lit. The party is at full shout now. Pigs, thinks Moira, smiling stiffly. Pigs snorting at cows mooing at dogs barking at sheep baahing at cats. 'Hello, Isobel.' Cow? No, cat. Neatly padded little cat with the flesh just right all over and too much of it showing up front. 'Moira! This is a wonderful party. Can I help? No? Really?'

The doorbell rings again.

'Moira, my darling, why are you so sexy? Happy Christmas with all my love.'

Howard thrusts a wet bouquet of chrysanthemums at Moira. He is wearing a Santa Claus beard hooked over his ears and a red pixie hat. 'Ho ho ho!' he roars as he makes to kiss Moira's mouth and gets her cheek.

'Howard. For heaven's sake come in. Why are you standing on the doorstep? It's freezing.' Moira holds the dripping flowers at arm's length. The petals are already beginning to fall. The wind has come up and the snow is driving in, falling on the indoor mat. 'Is there someone behind you?'

'Well, yes, actually. You see, I was having dinner with Sheila.'

'Howard, I told you Kate would be here.'

The Sheila thing tugs at Howard's sleeve.

'I think we ought to go. Honestly, Howard. Sorry, Moira.'

What the hell.

'Oh, come in. Now you're here you might as well. But please, Howard, lay off Kate. She's upset already.'

'Bless you, love. Promise. I come in disguise, you see.' Howard grins and tugs his beard. He slips in before Moira can change her mind. In tow he has Sheila. She is done up like some kind of Santa's daughter, in a minimal black leather skirt and sequined sweatshirt, white fake fur round her neck and frosted Christmas balls worn as earrings. She has Kate's raven hair brushed not down but up into two hopeful

110

bunches. From each bunch hangs a silver star. Perhaps she is not Santa's daughter but a Christmas tree?

Howard presents her as if he had breathed upon clay and made her.

'Moira, love, this is Sheila. Sheila, Moira.'

'Hello, Sheila. Please. Coats over there then help yourself. You know the way, Howard.'

In the kitchen Moira looks at the damp, shedding flowers and makes up her mind. Break the stems and shove them down the waste-disposal. One bloom gets stuck. She has to pull it back and pluck off the petals. Loves me. Loves me not. Loves. Me. Not.

She pours herself a glass of kitchen wine.

'Judith! You made me jump.' The last of the petals has disappeared. The voice of the waste-disposal changes from the tone of mastication to that of hunger. 'Sorry, I'll turn this racket off. Isn't it queer, it eats bones but not meat. Have a glass of wine.'

'Don't let me keep you.'

'Please. Sit down, if you can find somewhere.' Moira grins. 'I feel like the little mermaid who had to keep dancing though her feet were bleeding.' Her hair is coming down at the back. She shoves in a pin. 'Funny about Hans Andersen, isn't it? Fairy tales are supposed to have happy endings but his hardly ever do. The same with Perrault's *Red Riding Hood*.'

'Children like them.'

Judith has taken the kitchen stool. Moira collapses in the old basket chair.

'Do they?'

Judith nods.

'Children don't mind bad news. It's secrets that frighten them.'

'Yes. That makes sense.' Moira fills up their glasses. 'Of course, it's your thing, isn't it. What children want, I mean.' With the darkness and the kitchen porch light off, the window has become opaque. She thinks of the wicked magician's mirror in *The Snow Queen*, in which things that were ugly were ten times magnified. The loveliest landscapes became

111

boiled spinach and a good thought was turned to a wrinkle. 'Though I never think of children when I'm writing them.'

'They're very powerful, aren't they?' Judith says. 'Like myths. Perhaps they shouldn't be analysed. You know, I have sat in a seminar and heard grown men argue about the oral fixation in *Hansel and Gretel*. *Goldilocks* and sibling rivalry. But I'm keeping you from the party.'

Judith looks tired. Tiring job, Moira thinks, witch-doctor to children. Witch. Probing all those little heads. Taking away the toads.

'Lord, no. They don't need any more food. They're eating each other up there. All I hope is Kate and Howard don't meet head on. Or rather, Kate and Howard and Sheila. And I meant to ask about Minnie.'

I meant to ask you to take her away. Put her in a bottle. Throw it in the sea.

'I've never said how grateful I am. She's not too much?'

'No. It's just that she doesn't eat. That is, she does eat but only food she's stolen. Perhaps we could meet next week? Lunch or something?'

'Of course. Not that I know much more than you do. Just that if you hadn't taken her she'd be another derelict. If you can cope for a bit, I'm sure she'll be all right. At least, she'll have to take her chance.' Judith looks up. 'But it's you I was wondering about. You and Dan.'

'Don't you mean Sam?'

'And Sam, naturally.'

'You did wonders with him,' Moira says. 'Though I do worry. He's rather a loner. Almost a hermit.'

'And you?' Judith asks. 'Do you think about it much? Do you and Dan talk?'

'About the accident?'

'About Lucy.'

Watch it. Moira sees herself sitting in her kitchen in her red dress in the basket chair. Stillness is dangerous, you can turn to stone, sitting. There is her glass of red wine on the table at her elbow, a jug of orange juice, a knife, a loaf. Each object is complete in itself and yet part of the whole. The French call still life dead nature. So the still woman turned

112

to stone and although she screamed and wept and cursed, no one could hear. Failing action, break. Sweep the table clear so that the glass shatters, the wine spills.

'I'm busy. I don't think self-pity is helpful.'

'But grieving?' Judith is prodding gently. 'That's a long process. You and Dan – '

'We have our own ways of dealing with it.'

'Something like this is a strain on a marriage.'

If I could weep I'd cry out my eyes. Dan and I sleep back to back. I knew a woman once who lost a child and she talked and talked and spilled her grief in every ear. She wandered the earth from pole to desert and desert to pole, and in every street, at the door of every palace and every hovel, she sang her cracked tale of woe, until word got round the world and kings sent their servants to bolt their doors, villagers their dogs to chase her away. For her gaze was terrible and she could kill with a glance.

There is no happy ending to this story.

'I'm sorry,' Judith says. 'I've been intrusive. And you've got your party. If you still feel like lunch? After Christmas?'

'Of course. I'd like that.'

Moira takes two plates of stuffed eggs, Judith the last of the sausage rolls, to carry upstairs.

'I wish we'd seen more of each other. The four of us I mean, you and Dan.'

'So do I. They were good times, weren't they? Or that's how they seem, looking back. The summers.'

'Oh yes, they were. The summers.'

Moira carries the plates around, so far as she can in the crush.

Someone catches her elbow.

'Moira, tell me, who is that peculiar little person? Over there by the tree, talking to Dan?'

Oh, my God. Minnie, face white as a clown's, blood-coloured lips and hair cut into a fright wig, gazing up at Dan. Dan is doing his charming crane act. He appears to have enchanted Minnie. Moira would have judged her unenchantable.

'Just a girl we have staying with us.'

113

Moira has a not unpleasant sense of floating. Her feet no longer hurt. They hardly touch the ground. She switches off all those voices, accepts kisses from she knows not whom – some dry on the cheek, some wet on the mouth. In the dark, uncurtained windows there is a second party going on. It appears to be a good one. The candled tree could mark the edge of a forest. The faces seem softer, kinder, haloed, dipping and turning as calmly as rooted plants. The mouths are blind and the figures those of dreamers, among whom Moira glimpses a woman who is and is not herself. Who wears a red dress and her hair piled high, and turns full-face as though to speak and be recognised, when there is a shriek from the stairs that go up.

'Moira!'

'Kate, what's the matter?'

By now Sam and Donny have come out onto the half-landing and the party has fallen silent, so Kate has a full audience as she stumbles down the stairs clutching a screaming Poppy. Even Barney appears briefly beside Sam and Donny, his grey muzzle enquiring, but chooses discretion and pads away.

'Kate! For heaven's sake what is it?'

Moira catches her by the arms just as she reaches the bottom step. It could be an opera. The murmuring chorus. Moira and now Judith as attendants. Kate, the tragic mother with her child in her arms (now kicking Kate's stomach), letting go of Poppy only long enough to point one blaming forefinger vaguely upwards.

'Howard! And that thing!'

'Yes, I know Howard's here. I'm sorry. Dan asked him and then he brought her.'

Kate's eyes have never been so large or so brilliantly swimming. Her skin glows with righteousness and reproach.

'No! Up there, in the spare room! The two of them! Him and her! Her and him! The bed!'

'Oh, Lord. Oh, Kate darling,' Moira says. 'I am so sorry.' And thinks, ho ho ho to you, Santa. Meanwhile Poppy has returned to infancy and arched her spine so that her limbs flail and Moira marvels that Kate can keep her grip. 'Dan?'

114

Moira looks round for help. Dan is standing by the Christmas tree. His expression is both scared and fascinated. Min too is watching.

Afterwards, Moira remembers what happened with an awful, etched clarity. Awful because it was funny and yet it was not funny at all, when from the direction of the spare room Howard appeared, rumpled and with his Santa beard hanging from one ear. Behind him the Sheila thing was struggling to tug down her tiny leather skirt. She had lost one Christmas ball earring but still had the fake fur ruff round her neck.

Kate froze and would have dropped Poppy if Judith had not taken her.

'Moira, darling, I know this looks frightful.'

'It is frightful, Howard.'

'Well, yes. Then perhaps we'd better just slip off.'

'I think that would be a good idea.'

Halfway down the stairs the Sheila thing ducked her scarlet face and made a run for the front door. At the same moment Howard jumped the last few steps and would have sprinted past Kate when abruptly she unfroze, gave a howling screech, burst into tears and grabbed his Santa beard, pulling hard.

Howard yelled and clapped his hand to his ear. Poppy began to bawl.

'Kate! You're pulling my ear off! Let go!'

For a moment the two tussled, then Howard at last managed to break free from the beard and with his ear bleeding sprinted for the door. Kate would have gone after him if Moira had not held her. Instead she collapsed on the stairs. Moira knelt beside her and Dan hovered.

'Dan, get rid of them will you. Kate, darling, come on, come and sit down.'

'Moira, go after him! Get him back! Please!'

'Kate, stop it. You're frightening Poppy.'

'My baby!' Kate allowed herself to be led to the sofa. Tears. Shakes. Kleenex. Dan, having cleared the room, brought brandy. Kate probably shouldn't have it but it seemed to work. She pulled a face as she swallowed, then suddenly she was quiet, white-faced, and the shivering stopped.

115

'Moira, I'm sorry. Your lovely party.'

'Ghastly party.'

'We'll go now. Where's Donny?'

'Kate, if you want to stay.'

'We'll drive her home. Donny can bring Kate's car.'

'Thank you, Judith.'

So Kate is cleared away and Moira blows out the guttered candles on the tree and almost leaves the wreck of her party. But it will seem worse in the morning. Dan stacks and she takes one load down to the kitchen.

'Min. You and Sam go to bed.'

The girl puts down a pile of plates.

'I cut my hair. It looks horrible, doesn't it?'

'Well. Not horrible. But maybe it wants evening up. We can do something about that tomorrow, if you like.' Moira looks up from stacking the dishwasher. Waif or witch? 'I'm sorry about tonight.'

'Bad things happen where I go,' Min says. She does not wait for a reply. She seemed not to be expecting a reply, simply stating a fact.

Upstairs, Dan is slumped by the fire.

'Brandy?'

'Mmn.' Moira kicks off her silver sandals. In the morning she will find the food and ash ground into the rugs, the broken glass. Meanwhile she shoves a cushion behind her head and as she takes the brandy from Dan, feels the warmth of his hand and very nearly holds on. Remembered flesh. He has turned off most of the lights. There is a field of darkness between them. 'Poor Kate.'

'Poor old Howard.'

Moira feels faintly tipsy – the brandy on top of exhaustion. The violence of the scene tonight – however farcical it was – has shaken her more than she cares to admit. It was like watching one of those daily scenes of war on television. The viewer is at once horrified and thankful not to be a protagonist.

'D'you think I ought to ring Kate? Will she be all right?'

Dan sighs.

116

'Kate's a survivor. She won't bump herself off. It's simply that she doesn't acknowledge civilised restraints.'

'Maybe.' Drop it, Moira thinks. Every time we talk about the Summersons we come perilously close to confrontation. 'I've been thinking about University Row. Everything seemed simpler then, didn't it? Of course, we were all younger.' She stretches. The fire is dying. 'You and Howard were working on the hospital contract. I'd sold my first story. Sam and Donny were small. I found a photograph of us all the other day. It's out of focus and there's a blur where you set up the camera then ran to get in the picture. But you can see the garden and the swing. All that green. D'you remember those sunflowers?'

'What sunflowers?'

'In the bed. Between the yard and the apple tree.'

'We never had sunflowers.'

'Are you sure? How extraordinary.' Moira sips her brandy and begins to pull the pins from her hair.

'I don't remember it like that at all,' Dan says.

'Well, I suppose it was different for the women. You were working so hard. How's the Ridgely job?'

Dan shifts in his chair, pokes the fire. Sparks fly up. There was something he might have said but he changes his mind.

'Usual thing. You know, client problems.'

Moira is reminded.

'I forgot to say. I put a note by the phone. A woman rang for you. Fowler? Something Fowler.'

'Did she leave a message? Or a number?'

'No. She said she'd call back. Was it important?'

Dan shrugs.

'Just a woman at the Ministry.'

'Something to do with the problems?'

'You could say that.'

Moira yawns and stands up, pushing her hands through her hair.

'We're going to feel ghastly in the morning.' By the light of the fire Dan looks so tired, his cheeks hollowed. She wonders if he still has fantasies about that van in the lane, the phone

117

being bugged. 'Well, Christmas tomorrow. We can do as we like. I've only got mother to see.' She picks up her sandals. 'We haven't talked like this for ages, have we?'

'Have we been talking?'

Min doesn't feel powerful any more but a prize idiot. Everyone at the party was laughing at her. That's why the man was so nice – he felt sorry for her. She likes him better than the woman. The woman doesn't really want her, Min thinks. She thought she did but now she's not so sure. What the woman really wants is a baby. Min wonders why she doesn't have another one to make up for the one that's lost.

She washes the muck off her face. Most of it goes on the towel. She doesn't blame the woman for not wanting her. If she stays here the house will probably burst into flames. Something awful will happen.

You shouldn't be alive anyhow, the mirror person says to Min. You've got no right to be alive because Johnny is dead and you opened the door. You'd seen the big man before, the Provo man, everyone knew him, he used to give sweeties to the kids and he came in your aunty's cafe. He was a proper Santa, the way he liked children. The small ones used to run after him in the street, he didn't mind. Johnny did jobs for him, nothing big but it went to his head and Johnny was a real ass-hole. He must have blabbed where he shouldn't and the big man came to the door and you opened it and the big man had a nice soft way of speaking. Johnny was washing his hair at the kitchen sink. You opened the door.

Min gets the little gold scissors. She turns on the telly. Since the martial law it's military courts and they can hang you. They've hung two already in Long Kesh and there's going to be another, the man on the telly says, after the New Year. There's a little Christmas tree on his desk. He talks about Ireland like they always do, as if everyone's bombing everyone to bits all the time. Mostly it's just people trying to have ordinary lives like they do everywhere, only now they have to queue for food.

It's snowing in Belfast. And then there's Princess Diana in

the snow somewhere the Royal Family are, wearing a black fur hat and a red coat.

Min is thinking she wouldn't mind being Princess Diana, even though Johnny said the English Royal Family were all dirty fascists or something.

Min tries the tiny gold scissors on her wrist, where the scar is, but they are much too blunt to cut.

NINE

*H*appy Christmas, everyone.

Sam looks at his parents. They have put on a good co-production. Amazing, really. Dan has kept himself pretty well tanked up all day, he guesses, but he's doing well. And Moira's smiling a lot, being nice to everyone, the whole Mother Christmas bit.

The only problem is, having to look pleased back, as if you wanted Christmas and presents and it were all some sort of magic, as it used to be in University Row, before Lucy. When what it really means is eating too much (fatty goose, burned) or someone will be hurt. And wishing you could go for a run – run to the end of the world and leap off into another galaxy. And noticing that Dan jumps every time the telephone rings. And feeling someone in this house has a gun. Or there is a bomb hidden. Maybe in the Christmas pudding (which has dried out; Moira has tried to improve it by pouring over half a bottle of brandy).

The stupid thing is, Sam is really pleased with his presents – at least with the books, one on chaology with marvellous pictures, the other Mary Shelley's *Frankenstein*, which is the original story. But he can't show how pleased he is and doesn't know why. Perhaps it is something to do with those extravagant things they used to give him when he was small, when they always looked disappointed that he didn't scream his head off with excitement.

If he hated them or they were impossible, like Donny's mother, it would all be much easier, but he likes them. He just wishes he didn't feel responsible for them. If he could turn himself into a baby again, it might be all right. As it is, something is the wrong way round.

So when they open the presents, all Sam can say is: 'Thanks.' It is after lunch at which everyone ate too much, even though they didn't want it. Except for Min, who did her usual thing of pushing the food round the plate. But, so far as Sam can see, she doesn't pinch any food today and she seems pathetically keen to please. Sam still thinks she looks like a boring rabbit (even after Moira has clipped her crazy hair short and fluffed it out so it resembles baby hair and you can see her scalp at the parting). He'd sooner die than admit it, and he'll never tell Donny, but he almost understands about the stealing. He did the same when Moira was crazy after Lucy died. When he was playing truant and thinking of running away from home, he took an old camping knife of Dan's with a horn handle, a box of matches, a bar of chocolate, and a £1 piece. Nothing he couldn't hide. What he remembers now is that the thrill was not so much in stocking up for a quick exit, as in the actual taking of the things, knowing he had them and might be found out. Then they gave him Barney and he wasn't quite so lonely. Now he enjoys being alone.

Barney has been decorated for Christmas. He wears a red bow and pretends he doesn't mind. Within limits, he is an obliging dog.

Min manages to whisper thank you for the pale blue sweater with the white reindeer but when Moira tries to make her put it on she says: 'Oh no, it's much too good to wear.' Finally persuaded, she sits looking stiff and uncomfortable. The sleeves are too long but Moira goes on pretending it looks terrific. Then they pull crackers and Dan and Moira put on paper hats.

Everyone is acting. They have been acting all day. Then the early dusk rescues them. Sam slips upstairs and Min comes into his room. She likes the pictures in his chaology book, especially the golden strange attractor. She says it looks like a bird. She watches the film on Sam's telly, making herself so small and quiet he forgets she is there. He starts to read *Frankenstein*, flips to the end. He feels sorry for the monster. Frankenstein made him and then didn't look after him properly, so he finished in the caves

121

of ice. He must have been very lonely and scared. Like people.

Dan gave Moira a shawl. Moira gave Dan Mozart's *Requiem*. They yawn by the fire, to the Mozart and the bruised scent of oranges. Moira puts up her feet, wraps the beautiful shawl around her and thinks about her fairy tales. They are possessing her increasingly and she is beginning to make notes about them. She cracks a nut and grins. A woman has come into her head, who is wicked. A terrible woman, who in the street and the fields goes in the disguise of a good-wife, with a flower-sprigged pinafore and a yellow kerchief tied at the nape of her neck. She is known for her kindness, for the soup and pies she carries to the homes where sadness or sickness have struck, or hunger or grief. The troubles of all kinds the grey angel brings.

This good-wife is called to hard birthings and cold hearths where windows have been opened to let a soul fly out. And she never refuses, is never too tired and keeps to herself her wicked secret.

She who has lost so much is so good, they say. A brute of a husband and all her babies gone.

She walks quickly on small feet, her back straight but her head dipped in goodness, in her cloak of Mary-blue virtue. Only her kitchen knows where her babies went: sharp the knives, tender the last cuddle, crisp the pastry, great her appetite.

But her kitchen knows and waits and one bright afternoon as she chops and hums and cooks and smooths her pretty apron, the shiny copper pans fly from their shelves and beat her about the head.

The door flies open, on a bee-still afternoon a wind blows round and round the wicked woman. Her broom chases her, her bubbling pans dance on the range, spill over and scald.

'Pity! Pity!' the wicked woman cries and she runs from the angry kitchen, out into the street, through the village, followed by pots, pans, broom, knives.

Then the world knows her wickedness, for her pots and pans shout it for all to hear, and while the people dash from

122

their doors in rage, dogs escape their chains, cats and rats run after her, wolves come from the fields, and the woman runs and runs.

She runs to the end of the world, where she meets Brother Death and Sister Spite, and all three link hands and dance. They dance in the snow at the end of the world and at the sight of them around the last bonfire on the last ice-floe, pots, pans, broom and knives pause in the mid-air, then fall upon people, dogs, cats, rats and wolves. Man turns knife upon wife. Cat jumps screeching into boiling pot. And so they fight and run in terror away, away from the Dancers who laugh so wildly the Pole itself shakes.

Only one man returns, blind and bleeding but with voice enough to tell the world.

That wickedness always wins.

Moira yawns. That was a queer one. Why is there always a damn kitchen? And what is she doing with these stories, she wonders? I could be running away. But it feels more as though I were working towards something. I am not sure I want to get there, to see it, to go to the end of the world.

She feels cold, as though waking from a sleep. Perhaps she was asleep. Or going down with the bug. She pulls the beautiful shawl – thin wool, deep jewel colours, patterned with wonderful birds – closer around her. That is a comfort. So is the fire.

Not the *Requiem*, now coming to its sombre end. It is a piece of music that Moira has always found threatening. This is Mozart talking not about peace, but death.

Dan's gone out.

(Lucy was floating face upwards. One arm was flung back as in sleep. Usually she slept like that, with the other fist across her mouth. Of course, she could not swim, not at twelve months, so she must have drowned quickly, to be floating. Her eyes were open. Beneath the eyes, as with so many infants, the skin was thin, the palest violet. Dan jumped in to help, I must have shrieked, but I wouldn't let him, we had this ridiculous struggle in the water, I was trying to hold Lucy and to beat him off. In the water we grappled like

123

dreamers with those terrible slow movements of dreamers: leaden, as you run in a dream through an invisible, resistant element.

Thirteen months ago, water would have been her element. She was conceived in it, that evening we made love in the new pool. On the scan-screen I saw her, treading the amniotic fluid. A creature of the seas. An early form of life. The whole of evolution re-enacted in those nine months. The gills. The water-flower hands, putative, wondering what to be. Then the tide went out and here the evolutionary parallel breaks down. Too abruptly beached, gasping for air. Such a short time to learn to breathe.

I see all this from a great distance, through the eyes of the stone woman. Once upon a time I was that woman and she is still my sister. She alarms me, I run from her. But then I am glad when she lends me her eyes or I could not bear to see.

I cannot bear.)

Moira cannot shake off the feeling of cold. She warms herself in front of the fire but she is still shivering. In the empty chair Dan has left his imprint on the cushion he puts in the small of his back. Husband. Love. The words are pebbles in her mouth. She turns them with her tongue. No taste.

And fragments of the wicked magician's mirror flew about in the air. And some received splinters in their hearts and their hearts became cold and hard, like ice.

The room is dark except where the fire spreads its fingers. Snow falls outside. The telephone rings.

Moira turns on her desk lamp. There are sticky rings on the desk surface from last night's party.

'I'm sorry, he's out.'

She writes down the name again and this time, the number. Then she sits at her desk for a while. What kind of business problem would telephone on Christmas Day? Moira thinks about Dan and women. Isobel? Hardly. If he had, Isobel would not look so hungry.

Moira rummages in her drawer for cigarettes. Empty packet. Horseman didn't turn up last night, which reminds her of something. Horseman's nurse, receptionist, whatever

124

she is – Brigette, Brigitta? Birgit. A summer evening comes back to her, when she rang Dan's office and they said he'd gone to Horseman's. And his receptionist said he was away, yet Dan was still late home that night. Birgit, of course. Makes sense. Must have been. Dan and his limp, a loving nurse. Comfort. Probably over now, but it's a shock all the same. Moira does not know what she feels about it, except to wonder if everyone knew.

Only four o'clock. Time to get to the hospital. It would be unthinkable not to go on Christmas Day. Moira surveys her desk. She rubs at the sticky rings with a Kleenex from the drawer and then she notices: her snowstorm paperweight is missing. She probably pushed it away herself before the party to make room for glasses. All the same it disturbs her that it is not in its place. Things have a mythic power. Ancient tribes worshipped trees, stones – not any tree or any stone but certain trees and stones: those they chose to invest with power. I remember I wouldn't be parted from the paperweight. I thought it was magical and it has kept some innocence, all this time.

That could be what Dan is up to, with his plans for new burglar alarms, voice response control, his sensitive electric and electronic systems. He is worshipping a power, calling it up to make his house safe, keep the wolves at bay. (It can't, of course. The vegetable and mineral world is indifferent to our devices. The tree does not know it is worshipped. It gets on with growing, living, dying. The paperweight is an image only of a world. An illusion. Smashed, it's gone.)

Min says to Sam: 'Your father's nice. But they don't want me here. They ought to have got a baby. I bring bad luck to people.'

She is rubbing the scars on her thin wrists. It's a habit of hers, though she doesn't know she's doing it. Sam wants to ask if it hurt. And if she really meant to kill herself or was it like the games he played when he was small? He wants to touch the narrow white cicatrice.

Min is sitting on the corner of his bed. She always sits

125

as though she is ready to run. She sees Sam looking at the scars and pushes her hands into her sleeves.

'I'm not used to places like this,' Min goes on. 'I don't know how to talk to them.'

Sam wouldn't mind going for a run. It's stopped snowing. He likes running alone in the dark, even in winter – especially in winter because then no one sees him. He likes pushing himself until he's dizzy and his heart crashes as if he might pass out, and then the second wind comes. That gives him a kind of high. He feels free then.

But Min's still sitting there hugging herself. He's got this feeling that somehow he is responsible for her even though he doesn't want to be. It's like when they gave him Barney and he didn't know how to look after a dog. Only after a while he was glad to have Barney.

Regretfully, he turns back from the window.

'They're all right, really. My mother's OK.'

'I know. But I can't talk to old people. And I'm not what she wanted. They're all the same, the people at the hospital, that doctor your mother knows, they all want me to say something.'

'Yeah.' Sam thinks he knows what she means. They go on as if they're going to listen properly and think about what you're going to say. But they really want you to say what they want to hear. 'Well. If you feel like it, you can come with me when I go into town. Maybe tomorrow.'

As soon as Sam has spoken, he wishes he hadn't. He has an awful picture of trailing Minnie behind him. What he had planned to do was to see Sally over this Christmas holiday. She had been almost his girlfriend last summer. Now he could have Minnie following him everywhere. He might have Minnie for the rest of his life.

'I might,' says Minnie. In the door she gives him that pale-eyed, pointed-nosed look, half pathetic, half fierce. Being nice to Minnie is like feeding a fox.

Once she has gone Barney comes up onto the bed. It's funny how he's never taken to Min. Is it that he's frightened of her or that the dog senses she is frightened? Dogs don't like that, Sam's noticed.

He hugs Barney and flips open his chaology book. If he's going on with his origins of the universe project, he'll have to read it properly. It says self-organisation is the other side of chaos and that explains how life could have begun. These self-ordering chemicals got together and made beautiful patterns. The computer-graphics make it look so simple. It might have been like that. If so, something went wrong when people started up.

Sam hears the estate car pulling out of the drive. His mother going to see his grandmother. He remembers Moira taking him to a Planetarium when he was small. A voice told you all about the stars and the planets and the galaxies. He knew he was supposed to find it wonderful and he might have done a few years later. But he was too young then. He hardly saw the stars, he was so frightened of the dark.

'Mother?'

Freda looks smaller, somehow younger. Moira kisses her cheek. It tastes dry, cool. She hangs onto the edge of the blanket like a perching bird.

Moira had been alarmed. Freda's room was empty and for a crazy second she felt orphaned. Then they said she had been moved into the public ward for Christmas Day. Shortage of staff over Christmas.

'Anyway, dear, she wouldn't want to miss Santa, would she?'

Oh, yes, she would.

Ho, ho, ho. It reminds Moira of Howard last night. Balloons, tinsel, telly going on – *EastEnders* bumper edition, Christmas in Albert Square.

'We had Santa this morning and a pop star after lunch. I have received a small piece of hard soap in the shape of a rabbit.'

'Oh dear. Here, I'll get someone to put the flowers in water.'

'No. Pull the curtains.'

'Am I allowed to?'

Freda makes an impatient movement with her hand. Get on with it.

127

Moira is hot and uncomfortable in her coat, sitting on the hard plastic chair. She remembers what Judith said about necessary rites. But she cannot recall a time when she wanted to be in her mother's presence. It seems strange that flesh should be no bond at all.

'It's stopped snowing.'

Freda is not interested in the weather. She closes her eyes then opens them, fighting sleep. She is struggling to formulate something.

'Too much time here to think. Never talked, did we? Not really? My fault.'

'No. Mother – '

'You were an odd little thing, off on your own. You and your father, thick as thieves. I was jealous. You were strong. You've always been strong. I admire you for that.'

'You admire me? But I thought – '

'I know what you thought. We've always been chalk and cheese. Or cat and dog maybe. Different animals. No common language. Well. You'll be getting back. I should make your escape. We're threatened with a magician. Queer how they think sickness turns you into an infant.'

'Bye then. I'll be in soon.'

As Moira steps out of the hospital the cold slaps her in the face. Freda, looking so young, with her hair long, wearing a flowered cotton dress, walks down the beach to tell Moira that her father is dead. Moira throws the stones of grief into the water: one, two, three.

In her room, Minnie folds the reindeer sweater as small as she can and puts it away. She likes the snow-storm paperweight best of all the things she has. The snow falling on the little village, the pond and the skaters.

She lies on the bed where those two had been going at it last night. The woman's changed the undersheet and the duvet cover. The bed smells of soap, all clean, like the blue sky ceiling with puffy clouds someone had done for that baby who died.

Minnie's never done it – her mam would have beaten her to the coalhouse and back if she had – but the big fellow, the Provo fellow, showed her his thing once in the alley behind the car park. All the children knew about that, the girls anyhow. He gave you sweeties then you had to look at his thing. She was more scared of him than she was of the soldiers. The soldiers didn't bother her so much, not like people here thought. There'd been soldiers all her life she could remember.

Mam's in the hospital now. Johnny was her favourite and afterwards they took her there. They give her the electrical shocks. She wasn't in the house when the man came. In the daytime she worked in that shop where they sell the real Irish linen. On the telly here they think the Falls is a bomb-site but that's a lovely shop, Mam liked the job much better than the pub work in the evening.

The linen smelled nice and Mam had pretty hands. Small feet too, she used to dance so lightly. That's where she met Dada, in a dance-hall. He's been dead a long time and Mam doesn't know Minnie any more. She looked all blank the once she went to see her. It wasn't just the shocks. She was right. Minnie wasn't anyone's daughter after she let them kill Johnny.

Johnny was lovely, I loved him. When I was little he'd come home and say, which pocket, and whichever pocket I said, there'd be a sweetie. He was the laughter in the house, all the time fooling, teasing Minnie she was a raving beauty and his favourite in the world. When she was little she rode on his shoulders and she felt so tall she was queen of everything and no one could hurt her.

Johnny came out from the kitchen, his hair all wet. He was wiping the shampoo from his eyes with the kitchen towel. His eyes would have been stinging when the big man shot him and shot him as if killing him once wasn't enough but he had to go on killing him and killing him.

Minnie is still holding the snowstorm paperweight. It is warm with holding. On the bed, she brings her knees up to her chin and curves her spine until she can pretend she is like one of those pictures you see, of babies inside their mothers. She wishes she could remember. The baby must feel very safe in there, it's no wonder they scream when

129

they're born. And they can breathe without air, and swim around a bit, like creatures under the sea.

If she stayed like this, curled up and very still, she might be like the baby was that lived here, and she'd be safe, and she wouldn't be Minnie any more.

After Christmas the Middle East hots up and in the northern hemisphere around Dan's house the air feels frozen. It is painful to breathe in. It is too cold for snow, so cold that the snowmen in the deep suburban gardens on the way to town turn grey and weep but do not melt.

Moira watches shots of the Fundamentalist riots in Amman and Middle Egypt. We should be worried, she thinks, this is dangerous, but it seems to be taking place in another world of harsh, bright light, that might have been cooked up by film-men. Since England dropped out of history maybe our hearts have frozen.

Dan is in London. For a wonder, Min has gone with Sam into town to Donny's or that Black Hole place or somewhere. Which reminds her of the meeting yesterday with Judith Kraft in the wine bar near the clinic.

Moira had not been there for ages, since it was one of those town pubs shunned by gown, all dirty cream paint, slippery mock-leather seats, warm beer and a landlord who didn't even make a stab at bonhomie. Now it had been done over into what Dan called Brewers' Vic: catching up with fashion long after the fashion had ended for phony dark mahogany, metal framed tables, ornate frosted glass, buttoned red dralon upholstery.

Moira threw Sam's duffel-coat over the back of the chair. She felt a mess, she probably looked a mess. She pulled off her knitted hat and her plait fell down. Judith had arrived already. She was wearing the same long suede coat, with a soft jersey turban.

'Sorry about that scene with Kate,' Moira said. 'I never thanked you for taking her home.'

'No problem. By the time we got her there she'd stopped howling. I think she'd forgotten all about it. Kate's amazing. She always bounces back.'

130

'That's what Dan said.'

They talked about Christmas and Freda.

'And Minnie?' Judith said.

'Just the same. More so if anything. She hides in her room. Hardly comes down.'

'I've got some good news about her. Well, news anyway. But if you hadn't taken her in I'm pretty sure she'd have spent Christmas on the streets. You know that under the new legislation attempted suicides are eligible only for minimum income support – like Aids victims? And I think that may go soon. We're supposed to report them but I get round that when I can.'

'I don't know how you stand it – your job.'

Judith smiled.

'Mostly I see children, as you know. They can break the heart. The suicide rate is low. But they have other ways of dying – inside.'

Moira fetched the toasted sandwiches from the counter.

'So what's the news?'

'We've traced her. She comes from Belfast. An aunt there is willing to have her.'

'Belfast? She said she lived in the country.'

'Fantasy,' Judith said. 'Understandable. Her brother was shot in front of her.'

'God! Poor child. Who's going to tell her that she's going home?'

'I can, if you'd rather.'

'I would.'

'No hurry. Sometime then in the next few days?'

'Fine.' Soon. Take her away. Now. I am a little mad, you see. I do not have proper feelings. The stone woman and I.

Judith was saying: 'We see quite a lot of it. Survivor guilt. It was very common among those who came out of the death camps alive. Every case is individual, of course. It can happen to anyone who has suffered a great loss, even though they were in no way responsible.'

There is a blast of cold air from the open door. The lunchtime office crowd come in. Their voices are too loud.

131

(Lucy trusted me, you see. That was the most painful thing of all, next to the loss, the child's assumption that you can keep it from all pain. For years I dreamed that she was calling to me, crying in another room, and I couldn't reach her.)

'How's Dan?'

'Dan's very well indeed. In fact, I think he's having an affair. Probably not the first, I realise.'

'Do you mind very much?'

'More than I thought I would.' Moira traced a pattern in the dust on the table top.

'So did I. I remember.'

'You? You don't mean Morris ever – ?'

Judith smiled wryly.

'Oh, yes. We nearly broke up a few years ago. You see, we can't have children. We accepted it rationally but it was queer how it worked – like a bereavement. We needed to grieve together, I suppose, and we didn't.' She looked up. 'You've no idea how I used to envy you. Still do, in a way. So, anyhow, I worked harder, too hard, and Morris had an affair.'

'But I always think of you as in control. Unassailable.'

'Well, I'm not. No one is.'

Outside the pub they stood for a moment before parting.

Moira said: 'I think Dan's frightened of something. He's scared to death.'

TEN

The cold has worked mischief on Dan's ankle and back. The pain is spreading to the neck muscles too, just as damned Horseman foretold. He did ring the surgery just after Christmas and felt a certain glee to hear that Horseman had fallen on the ice on Christmas Eve and cracked a wrist. Probably on the way to the Franklands' party. He would therefore be unable to play the piano on anyone's bones for the foreseeable future.

A couple of months, said the receptionist who was not Birgit. Birgit, it appeared, would be absent for some time on pregnancy leave. (That gave Dan an odd feeling: as though Birgit had somehow been unfaithful to him, sleeping with her husband, getting pregnant.) However, if it is an emergency, Mr Horseman is referring regular patients to a fellow practitioner? No, no emergency. I can hold on.

As the taxi crawls from Liverpool Street to Soho, Dan savours the phrase. Holding on: it tastes right, it is something he has been doing for a long time. He has always been susceptible to vertigo, can't even watch scenes in films where the hero is clutching a piece of crumbling masonry with the street floors below. Cary Grant would certainly have been only a couple of feet from the studio floor but in the old movies they actually did it, he has heard. Not that it makes any difference. For the same reason, Dan has a horror of small aircraft. Irrationally, he feels safest (though never safe) in the middle bank of seats away from the windows on a large jet 35,000 feet up.

The taxi driver is lugubrious. They wait a quarter of an hour to get round Cambridge Circus. It's the sales but it's always something. London stops regularly once a week.

Dan puts a hand in the small of his back. Stretch neck muscles, hold and relax.

To let go – a terrifying thought but a tempting one. To spin off into space. They say you black out before you touch ground. When he thinks of space he sees Mozart singing, out there in the dark. He knows he won't jump. He'd never have the courage to let go, the only valour he can manage is in holding on, but it's a lonely posture and any moment the wind could pluck you off. (When he was starting out, Dan was sick after site-visits to tower blocks.)

At the restaurant in Frith Street there is a message to call Clare at home.

'Sorry. I tried to ring but you'd left. I think it's flu.'

'I'll come to you. What's the address?'

'I'm not certain that's a very good idea.'

'Are you still there?'

'All right. But don't get a taxi. Take the tube.'

It is three flights up, no lift, and Dan's back protests. Clare takes a while to answer the door and when she does, he feels foolish, clutching a paper bag of oranges. Ever since they last met he has thought of her in the grey cloak. She looks younger in old blue dressing-gown, the sleeves too long, her nose a little red, no make-up.

'Sorry about the climb. But it's a good view.' She walks with him to the window, a few strides across the small room. 'Portobello Road that way. But it's the communal garden I like. Look, down there. In spring you'd never believe you were in London. Doesn't look much now.' What snow that remains is a frozen grey. There are two children playing. Both wear red caps and jackets. 'Here. You'd better take off your coat. Why don't you sit down.'

'I thought of bringing whisky. But I didn't know.'

While Clare is in the kitchenette Dan looks around the room for clues. Sloping attic ceiling, dormer window, white walls, rough, cream slub covers on sofa and chair, small table in the corner that probably doubles as a desk, judging from the stacked notebooks, lamp and portable typewriter. Gas fire flanked by full bookshelves. Virago paperbacks. Doris Lessing, Sylvia Plath. All very self-effacing. And then a

log basket by the sofa, bright sewing tumbling out. One
painting, quite small, faintly familiar. Dan fumbles for his
spectacles but they are in his coat pocket.

'Is that a Gwen John?'

'Yes. That is, I think so. Unsigned and provenance un-
recorded so collectors weren't interested. I got it cheap – that
is, it cost the earth. Everyone says it's sad but I like it. It's
as if she just caught the girl at the right moment. You know
she'll be disappointed but meanwhile she's hopeful.'

Clare hands him a glass.

'White plonk. All I've got. Were you followed?'

'Followed?' (The van in the lane, the click on the phone.)

'That's why I said come by tube.' She indicates the sofa
and for herself takes the chair. Apart. So far, she is saying,
no further. 'Anyhow, I shouldn't have rung. No point in
dragging you in. I shouldn't really have said anything. I just
had the feeling that you were already involved?'

Dan is not sure if he is relieved or alarmed.

'I think I've been watched for some time.' Relieved.
'Couldn't quite believe it though. Thought I was getting
paranoid.' He wishes profoundly that he had brought whisky.
'And I simply don't see why they should be interested in me.
A few houses and a children's playground hardly seem to
qualify for the Official Secrets Act.'

Clare turns up the gas fire and pulls a feathery-looking blue
shawl around her shoulders. A grey cat comes in from the
kitchenette, is drawn by the fire but first investigates Dan.
It jumps onto Clare's lap and regards the stranger.

'Sebastian,' Clare says. 'He's not used to people. A one-
person cat.' Sebastian plops to the floor and settles, but on
Clare's side of the fire.

It is midday twilight. Clare switches on a small table lamp.
Dan is touched to see that her fingernails are chewed. Is she so
much in possession of herself, after all? He would be almost
glad of a crack in her composure. She seems to be checking
him out for something, in the way of the cat.

'Before I say any more you have to make up your mind
if you want to know. To be involved.'

To jump or not to jump? It's a long way down. Dan

135

looks away, towards the window, at the low, dull sky, the colour of pewter. It'll be dark soon. Have the beggar and his child found shelter? Dan thinks of them and of Lucy: the playground he sits in every summer on her birthday. That is his rite, his ritual.

For this project he has spent a disproportionate time on the specifications for the children's playground, working at home long after hours. There are all the usual pieces of equipment: crawling tunnel, swings, slide, sand-pit. But besides these, he has included tea chests, bricks, a heap of timber and, most important, a tree. He had seen the tree when he drove out to the site for the first time that spring and it had been central to his concept. Since it turned out to be in the 'cordon sanitaire' he has had to resite the playground. A tree will be planted there, to grow, but meanwhile he has designed a wooden tree, strong enough to support a tree house, tempting to climb. He may not get it through. Howard was sceptical but in his mind Dan has held a vision of a playground he knew as a child. It was a spot children had found for themselves, beyond a copse at the end of a cricket ground: simply a place where the grass was high and a tree grew. Someone made a swing out of a car tyre. They cooked baps of flour and water on a small fire. But it was the tree that was magical. It was a cause of illicit danger. It invited, and in full leaf, protected them. He still remembers the smell of the rough bark, the giant bole it took three boys holding hands to encompass, the green marks and scratches on his knees all summer. The time someone fell and they thought he was dead and wondered, solemnly, if they should bury him. But they had to bring in the grown-ups then. The boy had only sprained his wrist but they were banished for ever from the tree.

Clare is saying: 'As I said, it's not research, it's manufacture. Though even if it were inspected, no one could prove it isn't. A good cover, like the one at Rabta in Libya. Almost every Middle Eastern country is stockpiling chemical weapons. As you know, Iraq's already used them. Since the treaty the USA, Europe and Russia have been shouting about how many tonnes they're going to destroy – meanwhile planning like crazy for covert plants like Ridgely.'

136

'So what are you going to do? What would you want me to do?'

Clare has curled her feet up so that she looks hardly larger than a child in the big armchair. She reaches for the Kleenex packet by the fire.

'Sorry. I must look a fright. The bug's gone right through the department. Hope you don't catch it.'

'You ought to be in bed.'

'Bedroom's freezing. Better here.' She screws up the used tissue and puts it in her dressing-gown pocket. 'Anyhow. What they're going to work on is something called VX. A lethal dose would fit on the head of a pin. Even if you don't breathe it in, it gets through the skin. The birds die at once. You'd get stinging eyes, sweating, cramps, chest tightness, twitching muscles. Then there'd be vomiting, defecation and urination, then coma. Asphyxiation is the final cause of death. The funny thing is, vegetation survives.'

'So are you going to make that public knowledge?'

Clare shakes her head.

'No point. It is already. At least, the existence of VX is.'

'God. I didn't know.'

'If I exposed what they are up to at Ridgely, they'd just carry on, then have the press in. It would all be squeaky clean. Which is why the protest groups can never prove anything until the beastly stuff is used. And then it's in some third-world country and everyone's shocked and forgets.'

'Tell me, why did they put out the housing contract for tender?'

'To emphasise their innocence. Public relations.'

It is quite dark outside now. Clare uncurls herself and goes to the window. She stands for a moment looking down into the garden.

'Sebastian loves it down there. Not many London cats have their own jungle. He stayed out there for three nights last summer.'

She pulls the curtains and on her way back to her chair, touches the exercise books on the desk-table.

'It's all here. I've got something the protesters could never get their hands on. The MoD medical records on servicemen

137

used as guinea-pigs for nerve gas at Porton Down.' Clare smiles. 'I'd make a rotten spy. Pretended I had work to catch up on last Bank Holiday. I'd just finished photocopying when Security did their round. So I grumbled a lot about overtime and being late to meet my boyfriend. In the books I've got testimony from the men themselves. Several of them are dying. Convulsions, muscle spasms, trouble with their lungs. One is blind. Most wouldn't talk at all. They're scared. But I've got enough.'

She settles in her chair again and Sebastian jumps into her lap.

'Daft cat, sit down. So I'm not going to resign after all. I'm staying in the job. I've got a good press contact who's willing to risk it. If his editor will go along with it and if they don't find out and slap on a D notice. Whatever happens, they'll have to fire me and I'll kick and scream until someone prints it or they have to take me to court.' Clare scratches the cat under the chin and his body heaves with purr. She says to Dan: 'All I want you for is a witness. It's something personal. I've no family. I simply want someone I trust to know what I tried to do, in case something happens. What you did after that, if anything, would be up to you. And I would forgive you if you did nothing.'

Dan feels gravid, heavy.

'I could withdraw from the project?'

'Absolutely not. You're under surveillance already. You'd be amazed what they know about you. You drink too much. You lost a child. Your wife had a break-down. She writes fairy tales. You've had one affair they know of, with your osteopath's secretary. Your partner's just left his wife. You've got a girl from Ireland in the house. That was a blackish mark. I trust you, so provided you weren't followed, you can walk out of here and forget everything I've said.'

'I don't want to forget.'

'Good. You'd better go now. There's a back door into the garden, and a side gate. I'll show you. Get down, cat.'

Dan pulls on his coat.

'You know, it's funny. The first time I saw you I thought you'd go to bed with me.'

'I would have.'

'And now?'

Clare touches his collar and his face.

'It would make everything more complicated for both of us. You'd worry about me. That's why I told you – because I guessed you might be sympathetic but we weren't involved.'

'You're sure this place isn't bugged?'

'It's clean. I have a friend in industrial security. He went over it for me. I didn't tell him why. But don't ring me here, or if you do, don't say anything compromising.'

In the shabby dressing-gown, with her unmade-up face, she looks like a child: too young and too fragile to be taking such risks. Dan digs in his coat pocket for his scarf.

'What got you into this in the first place?'

She shrugs.

'Nothing heroic. I'm not up to that. No fantasies about saving the world. I quite like my job, I like my life. I suppose I just got angry. The hypocrisy, the lies. It's a very English thing, isn't it? The dirty secret covered up. Only nowadays they've got their covert army of thugs. Maybe they always had. Not that they'll bother with me. I'm very small fry. And don't worry – I'm tougher than I look.'

'I don't like to think – '

'Don't think. Go on now. And thanks for the oranges.'

'You should go to bed.'

'I shall.'

When she opens the door Clare picks up Sebastian and afterwards Dan remembers that sight of her, standing at the top of the narrow stairs, the cat in her arms. With the grey shades closing around her, she looks like the girl in the painting.

He makes his way through the garden, where the playing children have left frozen tracks, like skaters. Windows blink as curtains are drawn in houses that overlook the garden. Indoors, there will be fires and cooking and warmth and children put to bed.

139

Only when he reaches the tube does Dan realise that he has forgotten to limp.

Sam is running in the dusk. He passes that van that has been parked in the lane for weeks now. It goes away for a few days and then comes back, so it can't have been abandoned.

The yellow sun looks like oil. It drains away into the meadows by the canal. Sam's trainers are sodden, the going is tricky even though he sticks to the lane, and at first it is painful to swallow the cold air.

Then he gets into his stride. The moon comes up in the frozen puddles and he likes the crack as he breaks the ice. The bare willows are witchy, if they catch him they'll sting, but Sam runs too fast for them. A branch squeaks, a cow coughs. Sam goes into a longer stride, it's easy.

It was fairly awful taking Minnie to the Black Hole. Because it was still holidays everyone was there: Donny and Tiger Tim and Sally. Sam had wanted to talk to Sally but you couldn't talk properly in the Black Hole, it was so noisy and then there was Min, looking scared out of her wits, even more like a rabbit than usual. She stuck to Sam like glue and he could see that Sally thought Min was his girlfriend. She looked at Sam and waved, then turned away and started dancing with a boy he'd never seen before. Sam wondered if she was doing it on purpose, to show him she didn't care, but then Sally had probably forgotten everything by now. It wasn't as though they'd actually done it, after all. They had just gone around together that last summer when Sally had finished school and before she started work. There had only been that one time when they'd been laughing about something and Sally let him undo her shirt and kiss her. But then at the last moment she'd said no, he didn't know why, he probably never would. She wasn't a tease so it must have been something else. She might even have been a virgin. Not all the girls at school did it. Everyone knew who the school bikes were – the boys laughed at them behind their backs – but Sally wasn't one.

Anyhow it was hopeless with Min attached to him like some sort of Siamese twin, so they went off with Donny

140

to his pad and Min seemed to like that better. At least, she stopped being scared and let Donny give her a beer. Donny lit the paraffin stove and soon it wasn't so cold although the stove made the ceiling drip.

Min was always best when you didn't take any notice of her. While Donny was going on about how his father tried to break the door down on New Year's Eve and he supposes his parents are going to get together again, so everything will start up in the same old way, Min was doing a cat-like inspection of his pad.

She liked the mural of the mushroom and the sunflower and the stick people. Donny stopped yattering and heated up a tin of beans on a small Butane stove. He even had a spoon now so they took it in turns to eat. Not that Min ate much, as usual, but she sat on the damp bed-roll.

Donny was talking about some band that had asked him to join. He's not bad on the drums so it might possibly be true. Donny couldn't decide between that and the *New Musical Express*, he said. If he worked for both he might get enough together for a deposit on a Snake motorbike, though he doesn't want to join the Cobras.

'They're idiots,' he said. 'One of them was in a smash Christmas Eve. Just a kid. He was DOA.'

'What's DOA?' Sam asked.

'Dead on arrival.' Sam pulled a face, mouth open, eyes crossed, and Minnie made a peculiar noise, almost a giggle. So Sam went into the whole routine, clutching his throat and making death-rattle noises. He collapsed off the box he used for a seat, then he said: 'I wonder what it's like being dead?'

Min made Sam jump, speaking up.

'Dead's nothing,' she said in a tone of scorn. 'It's a lovely bright light. What you want to watch for is being fetched back.'

Sam said nothing. Donny looked at her with new respect.

Minnie cheered up quite a bit after that. They stayed on in Donny's pad until it got too cold and when they were leaving, Minnie said: 'Can you lock this from inside?'

'Yeah, got a key now,' Donny showed them. 'Found it

under a brick. It works. See? So I lock up and put it back.' He jogged with cold. 'Hey, coming back to us?'

Sam shook his head.

'Got to go.'

Then it was worse than awful. When he and Min got home there was a car in the drive. While they were pulling off their boots in the kitchen, Moira came to the top of the stairs.

'Min? Can you come up? Dr Kraft wants a word with you.'

Min's face closed up.

'It's all right,' Moira said. 'It's good news.'

Barney was in his basket by the radiator. Sam stayed in the kitchen. He made a peanut-butter sandwich. It was like the time when he was small and used to listen to the aliens talking, Urth-He and Urth-She, but all he could hear was the sound of their voices, Moira's and Judith Kraft's. He couldn't make out what they were saying. Then Min made a queer noise, like some animal, and he heard her running upstairs. Something terrible must have happened.

Barney was hopeful. Food? Walk? But Sam shook his head. He waited until he heard Judith Kraft drive away then he went upstairs.

Moira looked up. She was leaning against the fireplace, a glass of whisky in her hand.

'Hello, darling.'

She looked pale and tired. Older. Old. Well, of course, she must be getting old.

She took Sam's hand and held it for a moment and shivered.

'Oh, so cold. It must be cold out.' She pushed back the hair that had fallen over her face. 'What date is it? Is it Twelfth Night? We ought to take down the tree. But it's so beautiful.'

'Ma, what was that about? With Dr Kraft?'

'Judith? Oh, yes. About Minnie. They've found her aunt in Belfast and she wants to have her. So she'll be going back to Ireland. Not at once. Not until she's ready, of course. That's marvellous, isn't it? Only Min didn't seem to think so.'

'Where is she?'

'In her room. I think we'd better leave her alone for a bit.' Moira looked vaguely around her. 'Have you seen my cigarettes? Doesn't matter. I'm losing everything today. Couldn't find that snowstorm paperweight. This must be for the best, for her to go home, don't you think?'

'Yes. I mean, I expect so.'

'Sam? You do know I was trying to help her, don't you? I just don't seem to have done terribly well.'

Sam felt awkward. He didn't know what he was expected to say.

'She's a bit difficult to help.'

'Yes. There are people like that. What time is it?'

'About six.'

'I'll get supper started. D'you want something now?'

Sam shook his head.

'I think I'll go for a run.'

Moira nodded. Then she said: 'Sam?'

He paused at the top of the stairs that led down to the kitchen.

'Yes?'

'Nothing.'

Sam goes on running. He doesn't mind the dark nowadays and anyway it's hardly ever totally dark once your eyes have got used to it. From the lane he turns into the canal towpath that leads to town. The important thing is not to stop, even when you're gasping for air. The first creatures that walked on the earth used their ears for breathing. All he can hear is the thock of his own heart against his ribs and an owl calling somewhere. This is the pain barrier. If you can breast it the second wind comes, is coming, and you can forget everything you don't want to think about, as long as you keep on running.

What I must do is make myself small, so small they will forget me. One thing I remember from when I was a baby is someone – it must have been Dada – calling me Mouse. I can't put a face to Dada but I hear a voice: where's my little Mouse, and his feet on the stairs, coming upstairs. I think he was like Johnny, I might have loved him. They called me Mouse at school because of my name, I hated that. But Mam said it was Dada's name for me on account of I was born so tiny, not much bigger than his hand. When Johnny read me stories I always asked for *Tom Thumb*. He thought I'd want the *Sleeping Beauty* or *Snow White* but it was *Tom Thumb* I liked best. He didn't have to be saved by a stupid Prince. He could sit in the ear of a horse and tell it what to do. He was in a mouse-hole and a snail-shell and down a cow's throat and in a wolf's belly. But Tom Thumb was clever and tricked the wolf.

I knew I'd never be pretty or a pop star, so I thought I'd be invisible. No one noticed me, half the time, and if I really put my mind to it I could be in a room and they wouldn't know I was there. Except for Johnny. I've always been like a witch you couldn't see in a mirror. But with Johnny I knew who I was, I couldn't be invisible from him and I didn't want to be.

Now I'm like a real witch, the way things go wrong where I am. There's something awful in this house, I don't know what it is, it might be to do with that baby, but it's worse since I'm here, I know. The woman's looking sort of sick all the time, more than when I came. The man, he's scared of her and he's not here so much. She thinks she's trying to be nice to me but there's something else in her head.

The woman and that doctor have fixed it so that I don't stay here. Not that I want to, thank you very much. But I don't want to go there, either, where the big fellow is and Mam's gone and I opened the door. And I didn't call out, I was so scared, and Johnny's dead.

Aunty would get me for the money I took from her till to come to England.

And Father Byrne will be after me for what I tried to do to myself, the mortal sin. Though I don't believe it can be so wicked if you've no right to be alive. God he'd understand, surely? Not God of the nuns or Father Byrne but the real old man if there is one up there.

Just before they fetched me back I thought I saw Dada coming towards me through the lovely bright light. And I

144

was looking for Johnny but they wouldn't let me go, even though they don't want me.

They're hanging another in Long Kesh on New Year's Day, it was on the telly. He's been on hunger strike so they're forcing stuff with vitamins down his throat to make him well enough to be hung.

If I curl up very tight like this, I can pretend I've never been born.

ELEVEN

Once upon a time, Moira writes, but she seems drained of fairy tales, of any stories at all.

She wears a long grey skirt with an old sweater and Dan's beautiful shawl, so warm, so soft you could pull it through the keyhole, so much too beautiful for her.

She lets her hair hang down loose, a frizzy triangle, just a brush pulled through it, and looks out at the garden, there, under the conifer, where the lawn slopes upwards and in a mild winter snowdrops would already be pushing through. A good site for the stone woman in that pointy blue shadow. Or would even stone crack in this cold?

And all they found was a heart made of lead.

Birds peck out my eyes.

Moira is lost without her stories. She has become a vague shadow moving through the spaces of the house, oh, so cold, cold. A power cut has sent Dan's thermostat insane so she sweats by night and all day she is cold, however many wraps she puts around her, however high she heaps the fire.

Her heart, if she has one, is either breaking or melting. She fears the cold and the thaw to come, both.

She is not entirely aimless. She is thinking, working at thinking, in between blanks as wide as fields of snow. It is heavy work and wears her out, though like some ensorcelled creature, she must keep standing, walking.

Dan, she thinks. He is frightened of me. Why? She looks at the frost on the window pane, for a message as clear as eternity was finally written in the Snow Queen's palace. But answers are not so simple, or only in stories.

There is the tree, heavy and sweet, needles falling, bad luck to have around after Twelfth Night. The little match girl

146

did not go in her grandmother's arms to Paradise. She froze to death in the street. In the paper it said, a beggar and his daughter died thus, in London on Christmas Day.

Apparently, there are sad, confused, possibly dangerous things going on in this house. Nothing like freezing to death on Christmas Day. But things going on, and I sketch in a response as though I were human, and it may be no one has noticed otherwise.

Apparently, Min refuses to come down from her room. She will accept some food but only if Sam takes it up. She will not talk, even to Dan. Presumably she says something to Sam. I've knocked at the door every day but there is only silence. Sam must have a secret knock, known only to the two of them. I no longer see her as a witch, a disturbing presence, I wish I could have done something, but I left undone those things that ought to have been done. So many things. I wish.

I go out to dig a hole for the tree but, touching the spade, cold iron burns, nothing will break the earth, nothing at all.

Dan is leaving me, in some way, I feel it, and can't reach out to draw him back.

I wish I could ask him about the woman on the telephone. When she rang the other night Dan was in his study and I picked up the phone on my desk at the same time. I had to keep on listening or they would have heard me hanging up. She didn't say who she was but I knew the voice. All she said was, would you ring me.

A bit later Dan waited for the film to finish then he took Barney for a walk. As far as the telephone box, I imagine. When he came back he kissed me and rubbed my hands. Dan is a man of great tenderness: I see him anxious, hovering. Lonely? Yes, he must have been very lonely for years. He is worried about the crack in the pool. He says there is nothing to be done, we'll have to wait for the thaw.

Moira ranges around the house. She stalks. She strips the decorations from the tree. The light is going and she sees her reflection in the black windows, a ghost in her own house.

She thinks of ringing Kate. (Howard's back. Kate is actually nursing the Sheila thing through flu.) As she plunges her hands into the tree the needles scratch the insides of her wrists.

Strong? Mother admires me because I am strong? She is failing now, systems packing up. And I never said: 'But all I ever wanted was for you to like me.' Is it always like that? Always too late? All those silences that should have been broken.

I sat beside her bed yesterday while she slept, in a weeping silence. Except that a stone does not weep.

One queer thing: as I sat by the bed I realised that only now, as she is dying, can I begin to see her not as my mother or my father's wife but as herself, a person. As she fades she is growing younger, soon she will be a woman of my age. So far it is no more than a line here and there, a sketch forming, a woman walking out of the mist. Soon she may be a girl. I can't work on this. I have to wait.

I went to the flat the other day to make sure the pipes weren't freezing. Maybe I was looking for clues, too.

There was the smell of her. On the glass-covered dressing-table the Coty's Chypre in the old-fashioned scent bottle, the ring-tree. In the small sitting-room with the view of the garden, a half-worked tapestry she had never had the patience to finish.

I always thought she was impatient with me (chalk and cheese, she said, cat and dog) but that was the infant speaking, bawling in rage for undivided love, instant, passionate attention. That solipsistic creature that never really dies in any of us. Now I think I see: she had a dashing soul that had nothing to do with me. I looked in drawers and cupboards for clues but there were none, in fact the whole place was extraordinarily empty of the stuff most of us collect, the baggage of life.

She was a great one for throwing out. Once a year to sales, Oxfam, dustbin.

Always ready for the off, she used to say, but she never went.

Moira sits in the grey pool of her long skirt, stripping the tree, and one of the silver icicle hangings snaps and cuts her hand, between forefinger and thumb. Blood. No pain at all but blood.

'Ma? What are you doing in the dark? Are you OK?'

Sam turns on the lights. Moira flinches. Sam smells of cold.

'Yes. Just doing the tree.'

'You've cut yourself.'

'So I have. Nothing.' She licks her hand, tastes her blood. Smile's a bit shaky but can still stick it on.

'You ought to put it under a cold tap.'

'Honestly, no need. It's stopping.' Moira stands up, stiffly, pulling her shawl around her. She aches with crouching and with thinking, thinking. Is it with Sam as with her mother: frozen lakes of silence? Dan's thermostats are beginning to mutter. Soon it will be hot as hell. 'You've been out?' Well, obviously. Neglecting rites, one falls back on devices. Dan's fortress systems. My fairy tales. Minnie? Was she just a device?

'The canal's frozen. Terrific. Everyone's skating.'

'Good.'

Sam warms himself by the fire. Moira turns off all but one table lamp. She hates those stiff, enquiring spots that stand around staring, like cranes with questions. Dan bought them but even he doesn't seem to use them any more. It is possible Moira could sneak them out of the house and break their necks.

'Beer?'

'Right.'

She pours the drinks, whisky for her and a quick gulp first. She settles on the other side of the hearth. Such big feet the young have nowadays.

She looks wonky, Sam thinks, definitely wonky. He'd planned to tell her he was not going back to school but this may not be the moment.

'I'm going to get curtains for this room. What d'you think?'

'Great. Yes. Curtains.'

'Sam.' She hardly ever drinks whisky. It's usually wine.

149

Dan's the tippler. What's going on? 'Sam, when Lucy died. I mean, d'you think much about her?'

'I did.'

'And now?'

'Just sometimes.'

'You don't feel guilty, do you? Because that would be absurd.'

He could just get up and say he had to do something, go somewhere. She never argues about things like that.

'No.' Sam shrugs. 'That is, we never talk about her, do we?' He brings up one knee and picks at a hole in his jeans. He doesn't know what Moira wants him to say. 'Is Granny going to die?'

'I think so.'

'That's awful. Well. I'd better go and see if Min's all right.'

'Yes, you'd better. Judith Kraft says they've fixed it for next week. For her to go to Ireland. D'you think you can get her down for supper tonight?'

'Doubt it.'

'What about Ireland?'

'She won't like it but she doesn't want to stay here, either. So she'll probably go in the end.'

And what was all that about? Sam hears the television from Min's room. Barney's been shedding hairs all over Sam's bed.

'Awful dog.'

Barney wags.

Sam thinks. Dan's in London again. In fact, he's hardly been around at all lately, not since Christmas. He's either late at the office or when he comes home he goes straight to his study.

Sam stares at the ceiling. What he really wants to know is if his parents are splitting up. He reckons it has been on the cards for some time. A possibility anyway. He realises he has been scared of this for ages, he's been watching for it almost all his life. Since the accident, at least.

With the cold, then the beer, it's hard to keep his eyes open.

150

He remembers when he was small, after Lucy died and before Barney, when he used to pinch himself awake because he was frightened to go to sleep.

All Clare had said on the phone was: 'There's a good show at the Hayward.'

'When?'

Dan leaned against the wall of the telephone box. They were supposed to be graffiti-proof nowadays but someone had gone to immense trouble with red nail-varnish. FUCK YOU, he read. He peered through the glass. Hard to tell from here if the yellow van was still in the lane. Just before Christmas, when Moira caught him watching it through the window, she said: 'Well, why shouldn't it be there? They're building that new estate between the road and the canal. They'll need telephones.' He had almost told her then.

Clare said: 'Tomorrow? It'll have to be lunch-time. I could get off early, I think. Midday?'

'Fine.'

Clare rang off before Dan could say more. Her tone was cheerful-sounding, brusque. Actually, it wasn't fine at all, he thought. For once the practice was working at full stretch. Howard was busy with a couple of domestic conversions, everyone was on the MoD job and the hospital management board was demanding a meeting. Fresh cracks had appeared since the cold winter set in. University funding had all but dried up and there was no question, of course, of government subsidy.

Could they really sue? Walking home from the telephone box with Barney, Dan thought he ought to call Howard when he got in. Their insurance would never cover a lawsuit on that scale. But then he doubted if the hospital could afford to go to law, either.

The truth was, he acknowledged, he would not ring Howard. He would evade this issue as he had so many others. Not grief, not the grieving for Lucy, but Moira's unspilled grief, he had evaded that.

There was his house, with the black-faced, uncurtained windows. Dan looked up at the cold stars and wished he knew them better. The brightest was Venus descendant, he knew that, and the Bear and the Plough and Orion's belt. But the rest of the heavens was a mystery. It was absurd, but he had a thought, that if only he could map the stars and the planets, he would feel a stronger foothold on the earth. As it was, star-gazing brought on vertigo.

Evasion? Commitment? Dan decided not to examine his motives in going to meet Clare.

Barney, already puzzled by this sudden night walk, was keen to get back to the warm house. Dan blinked, steadied himself, and followed the dog home.

Afterwards, Dan remembered Clare waiting for him in the windy canyons that lead to the Hayward Gallery: a slim, triangular grey-caped figure against the white wall. She looked not so much lonely, as alone.

As soon as she saw him she moved on, as though alone, and joined the huddled queue. When Dan came up behind her and spoke, Clare put on an appearance of mild surprise at seeing him.

Dan looked over his shoulder.

'Bit close to home, aren't you? The office, I mean. And should you be out?'

'Out?' The queue moved. They followed. 'Oh, the flu. I'm quite better.'

She didn't look it, he thought, and was about to speak again when a pneumatic drill started up. For the last few years several of the older South Bank buildings had been in a permanent state of decay and near-collapse.

Inside the door, Clare pulled off her grey gloves. Dan wondered why in winter everyone in London wore black or grey. Clare reached for her purse from a shoulder-bag Dan had not seen her carry before.

He had not taken in the posters.

'What's the show?'

Clare smiled.

'Winter sales sort of stuff. There's never much after Christmas. Gwen John, but not all the best and not many. Usual problems, I gather – funding.'

152

They followed the flow through the gallery. Clare seemed in no hurry. She paused here and there, looked and now and then nodded to herself.

'Sad,' Dan said. 'Sad lady.'

'Yes, I'm not sure why I like her so much. A sort of peace, stillness. I think she was brave. It's as though she'd come into the wrong world, somehow, or through the wrong door. Her painting was her courage. She was batty about cats, did you know? And always losing them. There are all kinds of stories.' In a lower voice, she said: 'Thank you for coming.' She smiled and moved on. She was wearing the same red lipstick and scent he had noticed at their first meeting. There was a resemblance to the portrait she had at home but her mouth was wider and fuller than any of the Gwen John girls. And there was something less contained about her this morning. Tremulous was not a word that could ever have been applied to her. But she had put on bravado with the red lipstick.

Dan turned back to have another look at the *Girl in Blue*. When he found Clare again she was alone, on the lower level, in the last room, where the later work was hung. Girls in church, heads bent, faces turned away. Nuns. Cats. There was a tension about Clare's back under the elegant cape.

Dan thought she had not realised he was behind her, but she must have done, because she spoke while still appearing to study the tiny sketch.

'I think they're on to me. The bastards have killed Sebastian.'

Outside, the wind whipped through the canyons and tunnels, from the river, snatching up rubbish: paper, dead leaves, plastic bags, even one red balloon. A child ran after it but it made its escape, up, away.

They walked quickly. Dan took her elbow.

Clare said: 'Isn't it awful? A man and his child froze to death here on Christmas Day. Or it might have been on the Bridge.'

In the Festival Hall Clare found a seat screened by a feathery plant. Dan went to the bar for two whiskies and as he was carrying them back he realised what the music

153

was: the overture to *The Magic Flute*. Like the red balloon, it gave him an instant of pure joy; a golden wink of an eye from lost summers when this was the music they seemed to play every night. Moira had constructed a magic Eden from those times and Dan knew it was never as good as that. But the Mozart intimated it might have been.

'Crazy opera. Great stuff though,' he said. He drank down the whisky and wished he'd ordered a double. 'They can't have.'

'Killed a cat?' Clare said. 'Oh, yes. At least I'm pretty sure. A few nights ago. He just seemed off his food and I didn't think about it much. Then he went into convulsions. He died quickly, thank God. But I felt so guilty, you know? Responsible.'

While she talked, Clare was rubbing her finger round and round the glass. Then she drank and looked at Dan. 'It was them. I found a bit left over, liver, on the mat, and you see, I'm afraid I never buy – bought – him fresh meat. I don't know if they put it through the letter-box or got in.'

'Was anything disturbed?'

'No. But that doesn't mean they can't get in.'

'I am sorry. Truly. About Sebastian.'

'Yes.' She looked at her watch. 'Well, I must go. I'll start blubbing in a minute. But why I rang, is that there's something I want you to keep for me.' She pulled a thick manila envelope from her bag and pushed it quickly across the table to Dan. 'I don't mean keep. I mean put it in the bank or shove it over to a solicitor. Don't take it at all, if you'd rather not. It's just that my press contact is dithering and I'm not sure what will happen.'

Dan had pushed the envelope inside his coat.

'What is it?'

'Photocopies of the medical records and the testimonies. I don't expect you to do anything with them, I just want to know that they still exist somewhere. But you mustn't get involved.'

'I am involved. I said so.'

Clare shook her head.

154

'Things have changed. You're committed to nothing. I don't want you to be.'

She reached across the table and touched his hand, lightly; then his lips before he could say what was in his mind.

Out of doors again, Clare pulled on her grey gloves.

'Don't look so worried,' she said. 'I'm probably fantasising. Anyone could have done it. A neighbour with a grudge? Poor old Sebastian tom-catting among their fluffy virgins. I'm not half as important as I think I am.'

Dan said: 'I hate England.'

'No, you don't. Nor do I, or I wouldn't be bothering, would I? Go on now. Take care.'

'And you.'

Clare kissed his cheek then she walked off, almost jaunty.

Dan stood until she had gone, hunched against the cutting cold. He felt inside his coat for the manila envelope. He looked at the river and saw that the red balloon had returned from the sky and, with wind and tide behind it, was making its way under all the bridges, downstream to the sea.

Howard and Kate (and Sheila?) are giving a New Year's party. Well, not exactly a party, just a few friends in, and although neither Moira nor Dan want to go, to turn out on such a cold night, there are the obligations of friendship, inescapable rites.

'D'you think we should have left Min?' Moira says.

'She'll be OK,' Dan says as they turn into University Row. 'Sam's there anyway.'

'I wish Sam would go out more.' Walking up the short path, Moira shivers. 'What's going on with the Summersons, anyway? I haven't had a squeak from Kate.'

Dan shrugs.

The door opens on light and warmth and Howard, wearing an extraordinary sweater, red and wonkily emblazoned with the motto: LOVE ME NOW. There is an arbitrarily placed pattern of hands, so that it appears he is embraced by the goddess Kali. It is far too long for him and one sleeve is already unknitting itself.

Moira submits to a wet kiss.

155

'Great sweater,' Dan says.

Howard detects no irony. He beams.

'Sheila made it for me while she was in bed.'

'Bed?' Moira looks for somewhere to hang her coat. There never is anywhere to hang your coat in the Summersons' house. Why should they have changed? She drops it over the others on the banisters.

'With flu. But come in. Drink. Food. The girls have been at it all day.'

'Girls?' Moira wonders.

'Kate and Sheila, of course.'

Of course. Moira goes from the narrow hall to the small front room. She accepts punch, of which she suspects Howard has already had more than is good for him. There is popcorn on offer and the Sheila thing is passing round hot, peeled chestnuts. She is wearing some kind of green leotard garment and over it a minimal stab at a skirt: more like a red pie frill.

There are a few of their friends and acquaintances, among them the Krafts, and a gaggle of University girls, who make immediately for Dan. They always do.

Moira smiles, hears herself talking, answering. Leans against the bookcase, wishes she had not come. She is tired, tired, she trails behind her the grey shade who drew her own blood on a silver icicle. Once upon a time, she had husband and son and friends and a girl, a child, she failed to look after. Lucy. Minnie. Minnie? Where does she come into this?

Where's Dan? We shouldn't have left Minnie.

Tomorrow morning they will hang a man in Long Kesh.

'Moira!'

'Kate – you look marvellous.'

So she does. Her creamy cheeks look plumped and ironed. Her black cap of hair shines. There is even something different about her clothes.

Moira follows Kate through the archway to the kitchen.

'I like your skirt.'

Moira has said the right thing.

'Do you like it? Sheila chose it for me. She has such a good

156

eye. Moira, you'd never believe it. She's been wonderful, so good for us.'

Moira sits down on a kitchen chair.

'Katie, love, what is going on?'

'Well, you see, Howard was so sweet. You know how he can be. And he really was sorry about that awful scene. Then poor Sheila had frightful flu, so Howard moved back in and she came too. Then when she was better and she was so good with Poppy and everything, and there just didn't seem any point in her going. She did all this – the popcorn, the lot. Come on, let's have a drink. I wonder what Sheila put in the punch?'

Probably toads and snails and puppy-dogs' tails, Moira thinks. Kate has stopped bubbling and is looking at Moira earnestly.

'Moira, you do understand, don't you?'

'Frankly, I don't.' Kate's face falls. 'I mean, it seems to be working but there must be complications?'

'If you mean bed, I've moved in with Poppy. You see, I've been thinking and I decided that had been the trouble all the time. It's such a small part of life, really, then it had never been particularly good with Howard and me. So sexual jealousy was too stupid. You know, all that thumping up and down and squeaking? The truth is, I've never told anyone, but I used to worry so much about having an orgasm because you're supposed to, I never did. Sheila has terrific noisy ones and Howard likes that. Of course, she's so young. That's all that worries me – Howard simply isn't monogamous and I'm so worried he'll get tired of her and Sheila will be hurt?'

'Oh, Katie!' As Kate's eyes begin to shine and brim, a shower threatening, Moira finds herself laughing. Then she is laughing so much she is nearly crying herself. And Kate looks at her, at first doubtfully, then with a smile, then she too is laughing.

'It is rather funny, isn't it.'

'What's the joke?' Howard finds the two women hugging and laughing in the kitchen.

'Sorry, Howard.' Moira grins. 'Nothing you'd understand.'

Howard wonders whether to be affronted and decides against it. But he is still suspicious.

'Well, you'd better come back in. It's nearly midnight.'

After the laughter, Moira feels shaky. It is as though she had been crying, not laughing.

Midnight strikes. Dan kisses her for the end of the year, softly, enquiringly, on the lips. She touches his face and shakes her head. She thinks, how I used to stride out in the world. She thinks of her mother. After all, we did have things in common more important than blood. Yesterday I sat by her bed and held her hand. That is something I never imagined I could do. That must be something.

After midnight the University girls – Sheila with them – go off to another party somewhere. The rest stay on, just a few of them, round the stove. On top of the stove a chestnut pops. Judith Kraft is looking very beautiful, her head resting against Morris's shoulder. Even Kate is quiet. Mouser stalks in and surveys them all, seems satisfied, and settles in Kate's lap. There is a hush. The old year has gone, and this is a pause, as though they were waiting for the new year to come in. Of course, Moira thinks vaguely, how silly: there was no need to strip the tree, not even Twelfth Night yet.

No one says, though several are thinking, they're hanging that man in Long Kesh today. They do not talk about it because they do not know what to say, they are not even certain what they feel. This man has done terrible things, he has killed six people, including a woman and a child. A petition for stay of execution has been turned down on the grounds of insufficient evidence, so this ritual, judicious murder must take place. The state, whatever that is, has decided.

Someone does say: 'Well, I hope to God they've got the right man this time.'

'Another bloody New Year,' yawns Howard. 'I'm getting too old for this.'

Poor old Howard, Moira thinks. All those glimmering girls and you're the one who's fading. It's not Sheila's heart that will crack.

'Dan?' she says.

158

'Yes. Time to go home.'

They drive back in silence, the headlights feathering the tips of the hedgerows.

Moira stalks around the questions she wants to ask. Not tonight.

She does say: 'I wish we could have done something more for Minnie.'

Dan frowns. The driving is tricky. A new scattering of snow over the frozen ruts but not enough for the snow-plough.

'What could we have done?'

'I don't know.'

Min watches Big Ben strike on the television. Sam brought up fish fingers tonight and I ate one. Then I went in the bathroom and stuffed my fingers down my throat until I threw it up. I got on the bathroom scales. I'm not losing weight fast enough. It must be water. Our bodies are mostly water. While I was there I got some more pills from the cupboard.

Sam says Dr Kraft's OK, he likes her, but he's not the one they're going to send back. Anyhow, what does she know about people like me, with her posh clinic Sam told me about, where those rich Brits send their kids when they wet the bed. When I was in that hospital she made me do paintings and pretended they were wonderfully good when I knew they were rubbish. I don't like any doctors, they've got power over you. A doctor said Johnny was dead and it was the doctors took Mam away.

Sam's told me something he said he's never told anyone. I know he only told me because he doesn't think of me as anyone. So he said, when that baby died he thinks for a while they wondered if he'd done it. You see, he was on the grass by the pool not far from the baby so he could have pushed it or picked it up and dropped it in, because he wanted to be the only child and have his parents to himself. It happens lots of times, he said, more than you'd believe, but mostly the babies don't die. I thought it was one of the most stupid things I'd ever heard, but he wasn't really interested in what

159

I said because I'm nobody. But he did say, though no one actually accused him, he guessed why they were asking some of the questions and he felt awful for about a year. For a bit he even wondered if he'd gone mad for a minute and done it and then lost his memory. I quite like Sam. I know he doesn't like me much but he's better than the others.

I only stole the pills because they were pretty, a nice bright red, and I've got a knife I nicked when the woman took away a plate, after I'd pretended to eat. I've got quite a lot of things now but I still like the snowstorm best. You see, only things I've nicked are really mine. Mam would have liked those little gold scissors. I got the knife and made some cuts in that sweater the woman gave us, as if it was a diamond tiara or something and I wasn't a prisoner in this baby's room.

After Big Ben and some stuff about the New Year, they did a thing about everything that's happened since last year. Most of it was terrible sad and the stuff about Ireland was stupid as usual. They were on about that prisoner in Long Kesh and I didn't really know what I felt about that. If it was the big fellow I'd be glad. But it isn't and I feel sorry for him. And it shows what idiots the Brits are. Before he's cold there'll be singing about him and his name will be famous.

Then they did Princess Diana and the baby. That was better. She looked real great in a green velvet coat. I dream sometimes that's who I am, not that I'd want old baldy Charles.

So I turned off the telly and lay here curled up and remembered one of the stories Johnny used to read us about the goose girl who was really a princess. She had a horse called Falada, they cut off his head and hung it up but the head went on talking to her and the old king spied and knew she was not a goose girl at all but a princess, a bride for his son, and he put royal clothes on her so everyone knew. I'd pretend for days how I was the goose girl and how no one knew and they'd be sorry when they did, when I swanked down the Falls in my crown.

TWELVE

T here is a ghost thaw, like a false dawn. Everyone has become so accustomed to the cold, they are caught out. As they step outside, amazed not to shiver, their faces appear pinched, blanched. They blink before the weak, low sun, as though it were midsummer.

Strangers smile at strangers, point to snowdrops coming up greenly, even crocus. Snowmen in suburban gardens stand in puddles of their own weeping. Snow crashes from the conifers in the Franklands' garden. There are patches of bald, brown grass. The day Freda dies Dan comes home with an armful of daffodils.

Moira stands in the new crematorium outside town, her arm through Sam's, and wonders, is this what it is like when the icicle in the heart begins to melt, the stone woman to crack, this dull pain? I watch that awful chimney, Freda going up in smoke (that is what she asked for: the fiery furnace, the oven), and although there is sadness, it is not as terrible as it might have been. She escaped their unpleasant attentions and whatever the disease had in store, nipped off when they weren't looking. Gave them the slip, eh, she'd say.

Sam and Dan are watching me, ready to step forward, but I manage. (I manage to slide my mind away from that other place of death, the small grave I never visit, though I think Dan does.)

I'm not very good at mourning. There is something wrong with me (and at last I admit it). I don't know the rites.

Formally, we stand before the small arrangement of wreaths and flowers, but the queue is backing up behind us. This is a dying time of year, so we go out and there are Kate and Judith. It was good of them to come. Kate hardly knew her and Judith not at all. Kate steps forward and hugs me awkwardly.

'You OK, love?'

'Fine.'

As we step into the car Dan puts his hand under my elbow.

'You all right?'

I nod. We drive off. In the mirror, I can see Sam in the back, wearing his one suit, his face stiff, turned away. He always got on with her, better than anyone. All day there has been something reproachful in his attitude. My mother is dead. I should not be all right, I should not be fine.

I can't explain, can I, that coping and survival are not the same thing? That I am writing down the stories I had in my head, so far as I can remember them, and I am finding them terrifying. Something very obvious has struck me as I write: that, far from lying, fairy tales relate terrible truths. Cut the last paragraph – the one that sends children to sleep – and the wicked dwarf always beats the kind Mermaid. With the magic gone from the diamond sword, the poor Princess sinks down by her dead lover and dies herself, of a broken heart. Andrew Lang's Red Riding Hood gets eaten.

It is very dangerous to feel, that is what they say.

And perhaps I am getting somewhere, in my own way. Slowly. Through the stories.

I don't need Judith to tell me what they mean, all these lost daughters. But yesterday a new one came into my head, the first for weeks. Very simple, just a beginning really.

It was about a woman who loves her child dearly and loses her. But she cannot grieve for her.

O for our poor lost child, her family cry! What a mother you are, not to weep, not to tear your hair and pour ashes on your head!

But all the mother can do is to sit by the cold hearth.

You will turn to stone, they warn, and their voices are hard.

And sure enough, the mother looks at her hands in her empty lap and where there was flesh and blood, moss and ivy grow.

162

So they turn her from the house and the mother runs into the forest. Though her limbs are heavy as stone and the ivy now is twined around her face and in her hair, she runs deep into the forest.

There in a dark place she falls. But all the time she runs and even as she is falling, she calls out: Bird, lend me your eyes to weep! Beast, lend me your tongue to howl!

Of all the creatures of the forest, only two come near her – an old crow and a wolf who long ago lost her teeth.

The old crow says to the wolf: I am not long for this world. I will give her my eyes, if I may ride upon your back.

And I will give her my tongue, says the wolf, if you will be my voice.

Thus the crow plucked out his eyes and gave them to the woman.

And the wolf bit out her tongue.

Gratefully the woman received them.

With the eyes of the crow she wept.

With the tongue of the wolf she howled.

And as she wept and howled the moss and the ivy fell away and her limbs were light, so that she ran easily.

Where she ran and what became of her, we do not know. But there is a strange story brought back by a wood-cutter, that in the forest a crow who cannot see rides on the back of a wolf who cannot howl.

As though such a thing could be.

After I had thought about this story I was very tired. In the mirror my face looks cracked, my hair is greasy, ivy could be tangled in it for all I know.

And yet I am behaving well, I think. Well enough, so that no one notices, I hope. Perhaps Min – I thought I saw her watching me from the top of the stairs but before I could speak she was gone. And the part of me that is not wandering crazed in the forest, called to her but she didn't hear, or pretended she did not hear. If she had answered I might have gone after her and spoken softly to her, even put my arms round her.

Instead, I went into Dan's study and found the number scribbled on the corner of the blotter. I am not a witch but

163

there is a witch accompanying me who would make of this Clare Fowler a waxen effigy and stick pins in eyes and heart and breasts and bowels.

I must go in disguise. Tread quietly, carefully.

On tiptoe. Hush.

Sam has been watching. He feels like a spy. A secret agent in his own home.

Now he listens. No doubt about it this time. He can hear her voice, his voice, but mostly hers. War has finally broken out and it won't be a clean strike. As it escalates even Barney whimpers nervously. Not exactly whimpers – he's not that sort of dog – but he is disturbed.

It must have been like this for Donny all those years in the Summersons' house. Sam doesn't want to hear. He puts on his Walkman but takes it off again. He doesn't want to listen but he can't help it. Whatever's going on could affect him. He could be a civilian casualty. Usually he can hear Min's television but not tonight, so she must be listening too.

There have been signals for days now, Sam realises.

The first time I noticed anything was the afternoon we came back from the funeral. Well, no, before that, at the funeral, when Moira put her arm through mine. I thought she might cry, it seemed peculiar that she didn't at her mother's funeral. You'd have thought she wasn't feeling anything. I was upset. I was sorry Granny was dead and I thought the crematorium was horrible. I kept thinking about a film I'd seen about the holocaust and the ovens they burned them in.

But Moira didn't even talk about Granny. She put her arm through mine and left Dan out. He wanted to help, I could see, but she wouldn't let him. It was a bit sad.

Moira went in first through the kitchen door. I heard her say, Oh, my God, then Dan said, What is it, and we went in and we all saw what Min had done.

She must have been working all the time we were out because the table was laid as if it was for a children's party. There were great thick wodges of sandwiches heaped up. Some were peanut butter. Some were jam. And she must

164

have got a sponge-cake from the freezer. That would have been all right but she'd tried to ice it and the icing hadn't set, it was running down the side of the cake onto the plate. There was more doorstep bread and butter and slices of tinned ham just as thick. Standing on the counter there were the tea-pot and mugs, sugar in the cracked bowl and milk in a jug, along with a bottle of whisky.

And there she was halfway up the stairs. She would have heard us come in.

All she said was: 'I'm ever so sorry about your mam.' Then she bolted in her usual way.

It had got through even to Moira in her zombie state, because she called, Min! And started after her, to thank her I suppose, the way she is now you never know, but Dan stopped her. He said she didn't like being thanked and he was right about that.

Dan was right too when he said we had to eat it or Min would be hurt.

It was awful. Not being sure if Min was watching or listening, we had to go ahead. Dan tried. He made the tea, then said, what the hell, and topped up the mugs with whisky. In fact he poured away his tea and had just whisky. He said that's what the Irish do – they go to the funeral, then they have a wake, a real feast and a lot of whisky.

He and I ate as much as we could. It was quite hard to swallow. No one said anything. Moira was a funny colour. She took a sip of the tea and put a piece of bread on her plate. She stared at it as if it was a rat.

Then she looked at us both as if she didn't know who we were and said, I'm going to throw up.

I watched them. He stood up as if he wanted to follow her but she made a sort of flapping movement with her hands, meaning not to go after her. Only there was something angry about it, as if she was angry with him.

Dan told me to make sure Min was upstairs and to put something loud on, like Wagner. Then Min wouldn't hear us putting the rest down the waste disposal.

So we did that. We kept a bit of the cake and a couple of sandwiches and put them in the fridge to make it more

165

convincing. Min would never believe we'd eaten everything.

Then he said something funny.

'It's my fault, in a way. All this.'

I couldn't tell anyone what he meant. But in a way, I
knew.

No one knows, I'm fairly sure of that.

Sometimes I think Min might be that folded shadow at
the top of the stairs but she'll be gone in a couple of days,
anyway. Judith has the flight booked and Dan's paying and
her aunt will meet her. Dan's even said he'll drive her to
Heathrow. (Well, he would, any excuse to get to London,
a steamy thrash with Ms Fowler. He'd better watch his back.
I wonder, does he assume the missionary position for men
and let her do the work? That would be prudent.)

I do have other thoughts. Impulses, even. To tell the poor
child that I am sorry; sorry that she is not at home here and
she has no home to go to, not in the country, not with a swing
and a pony. I did ring Judith, who said even if she is making
herself sick, there must be enough nourishment going down
or she would have collapsed by now. She would never have
had the strength to make that terrible funeral tea.

As for Ms Fowler, she must be ex-directory. I looked for
the address to go with the number but she is not listed.

I have dialled the number that is scribbled on the corner
of the blotter twice a day for three days. I am not mad,
nowhere near it, but I need the voice, as witches might steal
nail-clippings and locks of hair. If she had answered I have
no idea what I would have said. Probably nothing.

Four times there was no reply. Once the number was
engaged. The last time there was a click and a voice of
sorts – a recording – told me that the number had been
disconnected.

After that false thaw, the snow is falling again. The West
Country is cut off. I smoke and watch television. Tempera-
tures above average south of Cairo, where there is trouble.
Trouble too at the Kremlin where the new guard versus the
old are fighting it out and whatever happens there will be

blood; but meanwhile the snow falls like a pantomime effect on those splendid onion domes.

I am glad of the snow. Its thick falling is the Snow Queen's cloak that felt to Kay like a snow-drift.

No one knows how I feel: that the carapace around me, the stone woman, is about to crack. I hold myself very carefully. I even went to the undertakers to collect Mother's ashes. They were in a small, plain urn in a cardboard box.

Most of my thinking work I spend on Ms Fowler. I have come to the conclusion that it will not be like Kate and the Sheila thing. Ms Fowler does not resemble me. She will be small, I think, I would be a giantess beside her. Her skin will be perfectly smooth, her hair the shining sunset gold of a real princess's. Put three little peas beneath twenty mattresses and twenty feather-beds and this real princess, Ms Fowler, will wake black and blue.

A snow-death would be too good for her.

Or drowning.

I sit. Sam is out. Min won't come down. Sam sat with her last night while she ate some of my good-woman soup from Christmas bones. He says he's heard her throwing up but last night she didn't. I sit. I unplug the telephone. I search Dan's study, every crack and niche. There is a locked drawer, the bottom one in his desk and not a key to be found.

I sit and watch the snow pause. The sky is the Real Princess's feather-bed. There is a slick of yellow light. I sit and look at the cardboard box. Mother hated sentiment. One place would be the same as another to her, so I take the box to the garden. I sweep away a patch of snow, I'm in a hurry now. Get kindling from the wood-shed, some of the smaller logs, paper, matches, quick, quick, hurry, fire, burn. The fire leaps, glorious, but it's still hungry.

On with the beautiful shawl. Much too good in any case, for me. It burns slowly. I push it, with its brilliant turquoise bird, deep into the fire.

Then the snow falls again but the fire has done its work. Mother would get the joke. Ashes to ashes.

The fire has eased Moira a little. For a moment she stood in the snow and saluted her mother's spirit. Now, indoors, she puts on a stew, washes her hair and sits by the fire to dry it. That is how Sam finds her, sitting on the floor in her long red jersey dress, with a glass of wine in her hand.

She's even laid the table and put out a candle.

'Hello, darling. I thought we'd have dinner properly tonight.'

'Great.'

She looks better but Sam's still windy. He ducks upstairs.

Moira brushes her crinkly hair in front of the fire, hears the static crackle.

She thinks of the fire and the snow and the story of the Eskimo child whose mother had died, yet she saw her spirit in broad daylight. And she heard her say: Don't be afraid, I'm your mother and I love you. For, as the story goes, even in that land of ice, Love is stronger than Death.

In his office Dan picks up the telephone to try the number again – but Howard comes in before he can finish dialling.

'Relief about the hospital,' Howard says.

'Not sueing? Yes. All the same.'

Dan shrugs. The hospital had been his vision. Its erosion distresses him. As things are, it looks as though, after the Ridgely job, they'll have to concentrate on Howard's side of the business – expensive conversions of desirable barns.

Isobel has put a bunch of primroses in a mug on his desk. They share a glassed-in hutch. The big room is dark, angled lamps nodding and dozing over drawing-tables. He remembers when they first did up this place, in black, white and grey. It was Isobel who brought in red wastepaper baskets.

'Fancy a beer?' Howard says.

'What? No. Not tonight. Getting back.'

'Right. OK.' Howard lingers, scratches inside his ear, changes his washroom towel from one shoulder to the other. Dan wonders vaguely why Howard has been working late the last few weeks. Not his style when there was a warm bed waiting. Of course, now the warm bed and girl to go with it are in his own home. Since Christmas his wispy beard has gone from sandy-grey to white. 'How's Ridgely? Anything I can do?'

168

'Give us some dry weather. Everything's stopped on site.'

'Right. OK then. See you. Night.' Howard manages a half-hearted leer. 'Flowers from the fair Isobel, I see.'

'Yes.'

At last he has gone. From here Dan can see Horseman's window across the road, a black rectangle. The new receptionist comes in for a couple of hours a day but the bone-fiend is still nursing his cracked wrist. Dan no longer gets much glee from Horseman's pain. He needs him. Since his last meeting with Clare the limp he had lost has come back, along with its fingers, crueller than Horseman's, twisting his spine in one direction, his neck in another.

He has tried her home number almost every night when she should be home, after seven. All the office will say is that Ms Fowler is not in today, can they take a message? In the daytime there has been no reply on the home number.

Dan shifts in his chair, looks at the clock and dials again. This number has been disconnected, says the new Telecom voice.

Wincing, flayed by the icy blizzard wind that has come up since the afternoon's pause, Dan uses his sheepskin glove to wipe snow from his windscreen.

Opening the car door, he feels on his key-ring the key to the drawer, thinks of the thick manila envelope he has not yet brought himself to open and read.

Moira lights the candle, serves the stew, takes off the Greenpeace apron Kate gave her for Christmas and joins Dan and Sam at the table.

Dan says: 'I like that dress.'

'I know. That's why I put it on.'

Dan notices the dress just in time and changes into a decent shirt and best sweater.

Sam notices that she is wearing a rather horrible scarlet lipstick. Even that might be all right but it's slightly wonky. Make-up doesn't suit her. She doesn't look as queer as Min did at the Christmas party but a bit that way, like someone in fancy-dress.

Dan says: 'What about Min?'

'Sam took hers up.'

Dan nods.

Moira says: 'It's a very peculiar situation, isn't it? Like having a fox in the roof.'

'Only a couple of days now.'

'Yes. All the same, I feel bad.'

She doesn't look it. She looks very bright. She fills up the glasses, just managing not to slop any.

'So how are the Summersons?'

Dan puts down his fork and drinks. There is too much salt in the stew.

Sam eats while he can. He concentrates on his plate. Something up. In America minors can get a divorce from their parents. They have their own lawyer, everything. Donny told him this when they were still minors. Not that Donny would ever have done anything about it.

Dan says: 'I think Howard's getting a bit of a bashing from his harem.'

'And whose fault is that?'

'I thought you thought it was funny?'

'Well, I don't. I think it's appalling and ridiculous.'

'Kate must have agreed? Howard could hardly have chucked her out of her own bed.' Dan has stopped eating. Moira, on the other hand, is drinking.

'Kate had no choice, did she?'

Wham. Zap. Even Barney has gone to his basket.

'I thought that was the point nowadays. That women have choices.'

'Kate is very vulnerable. You have never understood Kate.'

'You could be right about that.'

Dan ducks his head. His neck screams. The rest of the meal is conducted in silence. That is, neither Dan nor Moira finish their stew. Mouth tight, back straight, eyes shining, Moira clears the plates, scrapes the leftover stew into Barney's bowl, puts the plates in the dishwasher and serves Dan and Sam with baked apple. Sam eats. Moira watches.

Finally Dan says: 'Sorry, don't seem to be hungry.'

Sam has a terrible feeling that she is going to pick up Dan's bowl and throw it in his face. But she doesn't. He makes his getaway. Barney pauses to sniff the meat in his bowl. Too salty. He pads up the stairs after Sam.

Moira stacks the dishwasher and turns it on. She washes the glasses, drops one. It smashes on the tiled floor. She leaves it, but it is a disaster, a terrible thing. Heartbreak, she thinks, is this what is happening?

Dan has heard the smashing. He comes up behind her and puts a hand on her shoulder.

'Here, let me.'

'No!'

Dan has gone out into the snow. From the living area she can just make out his shape. He turns, as though scanning his house. This damned house. She can see him. He cannot see her.

Moira takes the last of the wine to the sofa, snaps on the television, pictures and words without meaning. Man dies in car in blizzard. Night of long knives in Kremlin. Civil servant found dead on tube line. No name. Weather: pretty snowflakes everywhere. Game show. Will the fat woman win the freezer? Sit com: *Them next Door*. Something about a lawn-mower and a jacuzzi and a meat-loaf.

She hears Dan at the kitchen door, stamping the snow off his boots before he comes in. He shuts the door. He's coming up the stairs. Quick! Turn off television. Beat him to bed.

But he catches her. He looks so cold and haggard.

'Moira, what's going on? What's all this about?'

Out there he has been thinking, remembering Moira's crack-up when Lucy died. His thankfulness when she seemed to be managing so well, all these years, all this time he has had to attend to his own wound, to mourn in peace.

And there she is, frozen rigid with some rage, in her long red skirt.

'What d'you think it's about?'

'I don't know.'

She looks like a witch. She is actually hissing.

'But you know Clare Fowler, don't you? You know her very well.'

'What the hell do you mean?'

Moira is watching herself, appalled. She sees the stone

171

woman breaking, prowling, picking up a heavy onyx ash-tray. Something beyond her control is happening, something that cannot be contained in a story, that cannot be contained at all.

Poor Dan doesn't deserve this. Nor do I. We should lie curled in each other's arms, I could go into his arms now.

'I mean all those trips to London to screw Clare Fowler. Telephone calls at Christmas. Is she good in bed? Is she young?'

Never borne a child. Never lost a child, Ms Fowler.

The room tips. Moira walks as though on a swaying deck. Dan puts up his arms to shield his face. Just as she throws the ashtray he grabs her wrists and the ashtray sails on. The black window will be crazed but not cracked.

She is sitting now, shaking. He crouches before the sofa and still he holds her wrists.

'Moira, I've never been to bed with Clare Fowler.'

'Let go of me.'

'Listen.' But she will not listen. 'The Ridgely job's for chemical weapons. Clare told me. She's taking a terrible risk. She gave me some papers. That's all. That's all it is.'

She is shaking her head: No, no. Wrenches her wrists free, rocks from side to side.

'A brandy? Come on. Steady now.'

In bed he lies down beside her. Side by side they lie, quite still. The storm has passed but nothing has been resolved.

Dan says: 'That wasn't about Clare at all, was it?'

'I don't know.'

I can hear them at it, a proper barny. It's mostly the woman screaming. I can't hear what they're saying but I'd guess he's scared.

It'll be the bad things I bring with me. All that rich stuff they've got and they're still unhappy, so it must be I'm like a poltergeist or something. Mam always said I was clumsy. Look at a plate and it would break.

Anyhow, I'm not going back. So I've got my plan and I'll do it. I'm not scared. Not half as scared as I am of the big fellow and my aunty and all the remembering about Johnny.

I'm not sure if I believe in Heaven or not. Father Byrne was always on about Hell and everlasting fire and how we'd get what we deserved, meaning the worst.

I know by Father Byrne what I'm going to do would be a big sin. But if the old God's up there, after the lovely light, he might see different. Johnny'll be there for sure. He could put in a word. He could walk out of the golden light and say, that's our Min – give us a kiss.

The morning is still and clear. Sam sees Dan out with a spade, clearing snow. He's done the drive and now he has started on the garden path. It is very early. He supposes neither of them got much sleep after the row. He wonders if they have decided to get a divorce.

Moira is in the kitchen sweeping up glass. She looks pale but not so crazy.

Sam finds Dan by the pool. From the way he stands, his back must be hurting. He shouldn't have shovelled that snow.

Together they gaze into the pool. The snow level has risen. It looks rather beautiful, all shining.

Dan says: 'Better fill it in in the spring.'

Barney has joined them. He looks from the man to the boy.

Sam thinks it would be a pity to fill in the pool but since it's just a hole in the ground he supposes they might as well.

Dan shifts his weight on the spade.

'Does Moira talk much to you? I mean, if there's something on her mind?'

Sam shakes his head.

'But I think.' He doesn't know how to say this. He feels very sorry for Dan. He's sorry for them both but Dan always seems to be the one who's left out. 'I think she wants to sometimes. Just before Christmas she mentioned Lucy.'

'Lucy? But she never talks about Lucy?'

'Well, she didn't really talk. She never does. I think it's all inside her head though. Sometimes more than others. And she can't let it out.'

Dan nods. It makes sense. It could explain everything.

173

And I haven't helped. But how do you force someone to mourn?

The margins between light and dark are very sharp this morning. The glinting snow and the inky shade of the conifers.

Sam saw it. He didn't. The boy stands in the cold. His wrists stick out of his anorak, long, bony, Dan hadn't even noticed how Sam had grown. Quite suddenly shot up, awkward, skinny, vulnerable. His face is all sharp planes.

'What about you? What did you feel when Lucy died? Can you remember?'

'Not really. But I think I was jealous.'

'Jealous? But Lucy was dead. How could you be jealous of that?'

Sam hunches his shoulders, kicks snow into the pool.

'It was stupid. I mean, I was sorry Lucy died. I still am. I was only a kid. I just had the feeling that you were thinking about her all the time. And if I was dead you'd think about me. So for a bit I wanted to be dead. That's all.'

'We worried about you.'

'I know. But that's not the same as thinking, is it.'

'Sam, I'm sorry. I'd no idea. That's awful.'

'No. Honestly. It's OK.'

Halfway back to the house Sam says: 'Does Min have to go back to Ireland?'

Dan is startled.

'Why? D'you want her to stay here?'

'No. But she doesn't want to go.'

'I doubt if there's any choice. Her aunt's offered her a home.'

Dan kicks the snow off his boots and hangs up the spade.

'I'm just going to the office. Want a lift?'

Sam shakes his head. 'Thanks.' He doesn't want to go into town but at the same time he doesn't want to be around the house. He calls Barney and lopes off in the direction of the lane that leads to the canal.

It strikes him that he has just missed a chance to ask if they are splitting up. And then he thinks, maybe that doesn't matter to him as much as it did. The idea doesn't frighten him any more.

She has become Demeter. A single look from her can kill, so monstrous is her grief.

Moira sees herself, sees all this: the witch-woman who knows that rage is safer than grief, so she will not have Dan's arms around her.

'Will you be all right?'

'Why shouldn't I be?'

She is set on war and nothing will stop her. She whirls away from him, chops carrots, slides them into a pan. She snatches up the Hoover, starts for the stairs.

'Here, let me.'

'No!'

In the living area she turns on radio and Hoover. The sun shows up the dust. So much dust she'll never be done.

Radio 3. Wagner. Very suitable.

'What did you say?'

He has to shout.

'Moira, for God's sake turn that thing off. I can show you those papers. Clare asked me to keep them. That's all. What am I supposed to do? Get her to write a letter?'

'No point. She's not at home. I rang her.'

'You *what?*'

She swoops with the Hoover, just missing his feet. Dan's still in his socks. He feels helpless and foolish. He ducks around her, turns off the radio and pulls out the Hoover plug.

There is a feral expression on Moira's face. As Dan pins her arms to her sides, she struggles, pulls against him, and as the wicked pain stabs his back, she breaks free.

So she is standing alone, crouched and panting, when Dan yells: 'I didn't kill Lucy. You didn't kill Lucy. She died.'

The first tears, though amazing, are not so bad. Then Moira begins to shake. The tears do not amount to much but she is winded, croaking for breath, every part of her wracked. She is hardly aware of his arms around her and when she does realise what is happening, she backs away.

175

'Please,' she says. 'Please go.'

When at last, reluctantly, he has gone, Moira stands by the window. She cools her face against the black glass. Her hand against the glass comes up against the crazed patch, where she threw the ashtray last night. And she wonders, whatever is it? What is happening?

THIRTEEN

A thaw is forecast, expected to be followed by flooding in low-lying areas. What with the drought summer, the hurricane last autumn, the earthquakes and biting winter, it is as though nature had run mad. Or, more judiciously, decided to punish the planet.

Meanwhile, Min is missing. She must have slipped out the night of Moira's outburst or perhaps the next morning when no one was looking.

There is a last, idle fall of snow. Moira imagines Min as the little match-girl, shut out. They will find her like that, she is convinced, frozen to death.

Considering the emergency, everything seems to happen very slowly. Dan comes home but there is nothing he can do, beyond telephoning the police.

Judith is there too, and Moira explains: 'She'd stopped coming down for meals, you see, so I didn't miss her until after lunch.'

'What did she take with her?'

'Just stupid things. Bits of stuff she'd stolen, nothing that would be of any use. She left behind a sweater. It'll be dark soon, won't it. She'll be so cold. I hadn't realised how frightened she was of going back to Ireland.'

'Pills? Anything like that?'

Moira goes up to the bathroom.

'She's cleared them out.'

Judith says she will drive around. She knows where the squats are. There is just a chance.

Sam feels awkward. Something terrible has happened and he might have prevented it. If he'd been that bit nicer to Min.

Then he remembers.

'I think I know somewhere she might be. We'll need torches.'

There is no key under the brick so she's locked herself in Donny's pad. But the wood is so rotten it's easy enough to force the door.

Sam points the way and they follow Dan with the torch. There is the mural of the mushroom cloud and the sunflowers and the stick people. A Coke can on its side on the floor, scattered pill bottles. And then Min lying on the bed-roll, her knees drawn up, her head resting on her hand. She looks quite peaceful, Sam thinks, as if she had just decided she was tired and wanted to go to sleep. Which is more or less what has happened. He remembers what she said when they were here with Donny: Dead's nothing.

He hears Moira's intake of breath and her cry: 'Oh, my God!' She kneels by the bed-roll, then Dan is pulling her away and Dr Kraft takes her place.

'She's not dead. Might be in coma.'

Poor Min, Sam thinks, didn't make it into the light, or not to stay.

Min is not in coma. She will not die. Saved by a small pool of vomit no one had noticed on the bed-roll. Dan found the snowstorm paperweight on the floor. It must have rolled from her hand when she fell asleep. Moira shook her head when Dan showed her. Let her keep it.

Moira is cold, so cold. Even in front of the heaped fire, she shivers. She has put away her rage, or it simply melted at the sight of Min.

The beautiful shawl is burned. Dan covers her shoulders with his jacket and takes her cold hands in his. A loving man.

'You're freezing. It must be shock.'

Later she looks up and says: 'I used her.'

'You mustn't feel guilty.'

'I must.' I must feel guilt and sorrow. At last I am grieving. I have to think and feel my way through this, Moira tells herself. This is not about poor Min, or not altogether. When we found her lying in the dark on the bed-roll I saw Lucy's body on the grass, Dan bent over her, trying to breathe air into those small lungs. With an infant, it appears you must be careful not to breathe too hard.

In Death's conservatory, in the fairy tale, among the water-plants, great palms, oaks and plantains, parsley and thyme, the blind mother could make out, by listening and hearing, the heart-throb of her child in a sickly crocus. She lost him all the same.

'Here, drink this.'

'Dan?'

You'd think such a loss would bring us together. It didn't. All these years I have been carrying a dead child in my arms.

'I'm sorry. It's been awful for you.'

He knows what she means.

'Yes.'

In the bathroom on the way to bed the pain strikes her so ferociously she cries out. It is like a menstrual cramp. Dan comes in and they hang on to each other. It is a matter not of comfort but survival.

Much of the time Dan and Moira are shy with each other, like actors who have left the stage. The play has ended and without it they are a little lost.

The thaw arrives, as foretold. Snow slips from the branches, the canal rises and covers the towpath. The remains of the bonfire are revealed and the ashes of the beautiful shawl. A few charred but recognisable scraps are left. From the window Moira sees Dan look, then bend, stir the ashes and look again, but he says nothing.

He is going to London today, he might be away for the night. He might not come back, Moira admits to herself, it is perfectly possible that he is going to Clare Fowler.

She looks out at the melting garden, the sparrows hopping among the crocus and tells herself a story. Only it is not so much a story as a moving picture, in which on a great, grey field people are strolling and wandering in a light like an

English winter dusk. They are alive, she knows, but among them, just as life-like, others move or rest or wait, and she knows them to be the dead. The strange thing is that although those she knows to be living and those who are dead touch and embrace, it is sadly, for this is not a meeting but a parting.

Moira goes through the books on her desk and on the shelf until she finds the Russian fairy tale of the *Little Daughter of the Snow*, who stayed on earth for a while, then she melted before the stove. But she lived still – carried away by father Frost, over the stars to the frozen seas where she dances all summer. In winter you might meet her again: build a snow woman and you may find the little daughter of the snow standing there instead.

That is, if you happen to live in Russia and believe in fairy tales.

'Sam? I'm going into town. Want a lift?'

Sam appears at the top of the stairs. He announced last night that he had decided not to go back to school. Dan said, leave it, it's not the end of the world, he'll probably change his mind.

'Yeah. OK.'

Except that she cannot stay in the house, Moira has no idea where she is going. Sam asks to be put down at the hospital.

'You're seeing Min?'

'Thought I'd better.'

'D'you think she'd see me?'

Sam stands with the car door open. He looks embarrassed.

'I shouldn't. I mean, you'd be wasting your time. You know how she is.' Moira nods. She is reaching to close the door when Sam says: 'Ma, you'll be all right?'

Moira smiles and nods. It suddenly strikes her, for how long Sam must have been anxious. Afraid, even. Children have a queer way of picking up the truth. Reparation is the word that occurs to her, though she cannot imagine how she can ever make it. Sam is no longer a child. It could be too late.

180

'You could take these. Pretend they're from you?' She reaches for the small bunch of primroses that have somehow survived the snow. She had intended them, vaguely, for Lucy's grave. 'They won't last long, I'm afraid.'

'Right.'

Moira drives on, into town, with no purpose except to keep going, not to be still, to fill in the time until Dan may or may not come home. The laurelled suburban gardens, bereft of snow, look shabby. And then here and there, there are splashes of colour: almost too bright, the pool of early daffodils in a garden, the dwarf tulips around the war memorial. February Gold and Maréchal Ney.

If it had not been for Moira's mad bonfire, Freda's ashes would have been buried in the memorial garden, just inside the new cemetery. Lucy's grave is in the old part close to the church, among the yews, longer grass and, in summer, wild roses. The paths between the graves are in places so narrow the motor-mower cannot get through.

Hers was the last in the plot reserved over centuries for children, and Moira crouches to read some of the older stones. Our little Lamb gone to God. Suffer the children. A grave angel with cherubs at his skirts. Moira pulls away the brambles and ivy to read one inscription: Woke upon the morning Light/Gone to Thee by fall of Night. That one must have been three months old when she died. One family, 300 years ago, lost four children in six years. Another, three in one year. Especially among the early stones, more invocations to Mary than would normally be found in a Protestant cemetery. And Jesus, on the whole, preferred to God.

Lucy's is simple. Name, date of birth, date of death. Marble angels are no longer permitted, even if they had wanted one. Not that Moira can remember what she wanted, or any discussion. As the sun comes through and she stands there she remembers Kate crying, turning to comfort her, Dan's white face, the sound of wood-pigeons, smell of summer. And herself watching dry-eyed, so there was the woman by the grave comforting Kate and the other, at a distance, over there by the disused pump, observing the ceremony. The crack-up came a couple of months later. And then the stone woman.

181

Very English, those rites. Excess is not encouraged, wild grief debarred. Sam, at seven, stands pale and puzzled, arms straight by his sides, fists clenched. Dan takes his hand.

And now I sit here. The sun fingers the snow under the mournful yews, sparks the intricacy of webs spun between the branches, warms my face though I am cold with sitting.

No need to beg for eyes from brother crow. I can weep by myself. If I wanted, I could howl like sister wolf.

Sam heard Dr Kraft tell Moira that Min was lucky, in a way. If she'd come over from Ireland and stayed in London like so many of them do, no one would have cared what happened to her. She'd just have died that time she cut her wrists. Or at the best, she'd be living with all those beggars. And a lot of them were mad. They'd just chucked them out of the hospitals and they were living like wild animals in the city. Even if they weren't mad it was difficult for them to stay alive. There was that one they found frozen to death with a small girl on Christmas Day. They were always doing programmes on them on telly, as if that made it all right.

Thinking about Min, Sam isn't so sure she was lucky at all.

When he asked for her they said she would be in the day-room. That was a bit of a relief. He didn't much like going to see people in bed in hospital, especially since his grandmother died in one of those beds.

Most of them in the day-room were old. Some were knitting or watching the television. One old geezer was talking to himself in a loud voice but he sounded quite cheerful. At first, Sam couldn't see Min and was ashamed to feel thankful: if she wasn't there he could just walk out and go home.

But there she was, sitting in a chair in a corner by the window, all hunched up, like a skinny bird with its wings folded.

Sam tried to give her the primroses and when she didn't take them he put them in her lap. They sort of bled, wet, on her hospital dressing-gown.

182

Sam was wondering if he ought to get some water for them and if she'd gone deaf and dumb, when she said: 'Thanks.'

'That's all right.'

Then Sam remembers, Min doesn't like presents, only things she's nicked. He'd sit down, only he can't see anywhere to sit, so he looks out at the view. It's nice from here: trees and sloping grass.

He feels an idiot talking about the weather but all he can think of to say is: 'The snow's nearly gone.'

Min gives him a look as if he were talking Chinese.

Then she says: 'I'll do it again. I'm not going back.'

Sam hopes she hasn't worked out how they came to find her at Donny's pad.

'And I'm not mad.'

'No, I know that.' Sam leans with his back to the window, jingles the change in his pockets. 'Couldn't you get a job here? In England, I mean, a hotel maybe? In London?' He has some idea that most of the chamber-maids in London are Irish.

Min pulls back her lips, tight, in that weird smile that shows her small teeth.

'Those old doctors say I can't live by myself. They can sign a thing to keep me here if I won't go to my aunty. But I'll get out and go where they can't find me. You'll see. Can you give us some money when they're not looking? Just to get there? I daren't wait for a hitch.'

'I don't know if – OK. I've only got a fiver and some change.'

Sam takes a quick look round, slips her the change and the fiver screwed up. He knows he shouldn't be doing this but he feels guilty. Telling them about Donny's pad was a sort of betrayal. He reckons people should decide for themselves if they want to be alive or dead.

'It's something I want to do, you see. Something I've got to do.'

Min can't say thank you, ever, but maybe she is trying, in her own way. 'And you're the only one that's understood, ever.'

'Yeah. Well, better be off.'

Sam walks away from the hospital, not looking where he

is going, thinking, if I liked Min, if she were even a bit pretty, I might not have given her that money, I might have tried to talk her into wanting to go on living. If I knew how.

At the bottom of the drive he stubs his toe, sees the bollard and gives it a hefty kick. That hurts. Good.

When he reaches the road he hesitates, then turns right. It strikes him that Sally will be back at work. Last time he saw her, at Christmas, it was hopeless because he was with Min and he had no chance to explain. Probably doesn't want to see me but I might as well look in at the shop. Nothing to lose. Why not?

Passing the sign that says HOSPITAL SLOW, Sam thinks of hitching but he is on the wrong side of the road for the traffic to town. He begins to trot.

The first thing Moira notices is that Barney is barking. He wants her to follow, up the stairs from the kitchen to the first floor. Then she sees what has happened and at the same moment the telephone rings. She stumbles against an overturned chair and goes back to the door to switch on the light. Then she answers the telephone.

'Dan! Thank God. Where are you?'

'London. Just to say I'll be back tonight. Moira, what's wrong? Are you OK?'

'Yes, I'm fine. I think.' Winded, Moira sits on the edge of Dan's desk. Drawers dumped on the floor. Papers everywhere. Wastepaper basket emptied and left on its side. 'But we seem to have been done over. Burgled, whatever. I just got in. I haven't been upstairs yet but it's chaos here. It's awful – as if they were trying to smash everything. I'll call the police now. When will you be back?'

'Moira, listen. Don't call the police. I'm getting the next train.'

'What d'you mean, not call the police? Dan, what's happening?'

'I'll explain. Got to run for the train. Check if there's anything missing. Lock the doors. Don't worry though – I'm sure they won't be back. Is there anyone with you? Is Sam there?'

184

'No, but I don't think he'll be long.'

'Good.'

'Dan, what d'you mean by they?'

'Later. Hold on.'

Moira checks upstairs. Here too, the rooms look wrecked. Dan's big grey and black oil painting has been slashed. The posters in Sam's room have been ripped off the walls and in the spare room, the old nursery, there is a smell of urine. She has very little jewellery since she hardly wears it but, so far as she can tell, a quartz pendant, an agate ring and her mother's old-fashioned diamond cluster are missing.

She feels she is being very calm, methodical, sensible. But downstairs again she realises that her hands are shaking.

Barney won't leave her side. She makes up her mind – they'll go down to the kitchen, lock the door and wait. First though, she searches among the broken bottles for the Scotch but only the gin is intact. She pours a glass, picks up the bottle to take downstairs and glances out of the window. In the dusk it is hard to be sure, but the van in the lane seems to have gone.

It was somehow necessary to explain.

They had made a kind of bivouac in the kitchen. Sam had done what he could upstairs, then got to work on his own room.

Moira said: 'I went to the graveyard, you see. Then I sat in the church for a while. It must have been longer than I thought. I didn't expect you back. Anyway, we've more or less straightened up the bedroom. It was queer. At first I was shaking – in shock I suppose – then I was angry. I'm still angry. I feel – assaulted. The jewellery didn't matter. Or the money. I think they took about £20 from my desk. It's not that.'

Dan nodded. He was still wearing his overcoat. The first thing he had done when he came in was to go to his study. Moira had watched him search among the papers on the floor.

'We'll get it sorted out.'

'I know.'

185

'They got what they wanted. They'll leave us alone now.'
Or will they? Dan thought. Photocopies can be photocopied.

'Dan, what was all this about? Why couldn't I call the police? What were they looking for?'

'Those papers Clare Fowler gave me. I told you about them. They were in the bottom drawer of my desk. It's all right, they've gone.'

'But this mess? Why?'

'To make it look like a burglary. Or a warning perhaps. Not that they need worry. I never even read the papers.'

'Well, better find something to eat,' Moira said. And then: 'Damn them. Damn them.'

In bed neither of them pretended to sleep.

Moira said: 'I thought you wouldn't come back from London. I thought you'd gone to look for Clare Fowler.'

Then she realised that he was crying, absolutely silently, hardly moving, just the tears running down his face.

'It's all right,' she said. 'Whatever it is, whatever happened, it's all right now.'

FOURTEEN

Dan is thinking of orisons and obsequies as he drives to London and arrives in one of those February springs a wicked March will surely come in to punish.

Meanwhile the early blossom is out in Arundel Gardens, in the private garden where he had seen the children playing in the snow and looked back at Clare, standing at the top of the narrow stairs, the cat in her arms, the grey shades closing around her. A jungle in summer, she had remarked and already the green is pushing through, promising August riot.

She had said he could walk out of there and forget everything but remembrance seems to him the last, perhaps the only thing he can do for Clare. Who died (or was pushed) early in the New Year, in the rush hour on the tube. It must have been on television, in the paper, he had missed it, they told him at the Ministry, the day his house was wrecked.

She lost her footing and fell on the line at Charing Cross. They were very sorry, a loss to the department, a valued colleague. Was he a personal friend?

He passes the street door. There is a new name by her bell and he goes on, round the corner, to the side gate into the garden.

Horticultural nature is often further advanced in London and Dan is standing stupidly among daffodils and long grass when he hears a sound above and looks up, absurdly hopeful, to see a woman, a stranger, shaking a rug from Clare's window. She is wearing a red scarf tied at the nape of her neck and, for a moment, shades her eyes to see who is standing in the garden. Then a door opens on the ground floor of another house and a young woman wheels out a pram. She puts it under a tree, where the baby will see the branches but will not have the sun in its eyes. There is a net against cats over the pram. Dan half-waves good morning but she cannot see him for the sun. He feels like a ghost.

Moira listened then said: 'What will you do?'

'Nothing. There's nothing I can do, is there?'

'But if they did kill her.'

'They did. I think the last time I saw her she was half-expecting something like this.'

'And you?'

'Well, I'm still on the job.'

This was the first time they had spoken openly of the whole business. Moira's tone was tentative.

'If you want to follow it through – I daresay you could get some journalist interested. I mean, in her death. Were you committed?'

'I thought I was for five minutes. But you know me – no head for heights.'

Moira shivered.

'Perhaps we should think of moving? Sell this house?'

The day after the break-in Min had gone missing from the hospital and as Dan strolls on the South Bank by the river he is half-looking for her. He buys a small posy of violets from the flower-seller outside the Festival Hall. In the spring sunshine by Hungerford Bridge two small girls, beggars' children, are playing some game of their own invention, hopping over the cracks in the paving-stones and singing a song, the words of which sound vaguely familiar. Dan listens then remembers: Don't-care didn't care/Don't-care was wild/Don't-care stole plum and pear/Like any beggar's child.

One catches him watching them and for a second, as she looks up, Dan sees in her face, vertiginously, Lucy and Min and that other beggar's daughter and her boy father.

Then the child pushes out her hand: 'Give us yer change, mister.'

At the middle of the bridge he pauses. He thinks of Clare in her grey cloak and of the red balloon. Above him a train rattles past. Below, the river traffic is kicking up the placid

188

water into a shining fuss of small waves. A sight-seeing water-bus passes beneath the bridge and carries away Dan's violets in its shadowed wake.

Step by step, Moira goes, day by day.

At first Kate comes to help her sort the chaos in the house, puzzled that the police have not been called, if only to be sure of insurance. Moira says they can't be bothered, nothing of value has been damaged. Sam and Donny do the heavy work. Dan has talked to Sam about leaving school and a compromise has been reached. He will take a year off, join the band of the young who can be seen now in almost any part of the world, today's vagantes back-packing as far as their money will stretch. Then maybe sixth-form college. He is seeing a lot of Sally lately.

Then Moira wants to work alone. She drives to the DIY hypermarket, stocks up and finds she is enjoying the pattern to her days, scrubbing down, painting. She digs out the best photograph of Lucy and puts it up. She paints over the blue sky and puffy white clouds on the nursery ceiling.

She can think about Lucy now. She can even talk of her to Dan and for the first time, in a sense, they are mourning together. There is no cure, Moira knows that, time will not heal, but something necessary has happened: that raging madness, as she sees it.

She has a feeling that that monstrous grief will not come back. But there is nothing certain.

Meanwhile, she works. She flings open the windows to let out the smell of paint and sees that there is a pink haze on the trees. They have started digging for the estate over there, by the lane. Has that yellow van gone for good? Or will they wonder for a long time yet if the phone is bugged, if Dan is followed?

She can talk about Clare Fowler now.

'Did she have any family? There must have been a funeral?'

Dan says: 'She told me she had no one. But the woman at the Ministry mentioned a brother from abroad.'

'No point in trying to trace him?'

'To tell him his sister was murdered? Without evidence?'

189

'No, I suppose not. And you don't know where the originals are? Of the photocopies you had?'

'No. And I don't think I want to.'

Dan is working at the board in his study. Moira looks over his shoulder.

'What's that?'

'An elevation for the playground at Ridgely.' He explains it to her. 'And in the middle there, you see, a climbing tree.'

'It's lovely.'

Sam thinks about Min quite often, if she's dead as she wanted to be or still alive somewhere.

He knows Moira feels guilty that they didn't manage to help her, didn't take more trouble, but in his view there are people you can't help, and Min was one of them. They didn't do her any actual harm and there were a few things she seemed to enjoy – like the Christmas tree.

He watches the television news from Ireland every time it's on, if he is at home. For about a month they are reporting on the night riots against the curfew. It is like some sort of goblin-land, where shadows run between fires, crouched, dodging. A couple of times Sam thinks he sees her, as a face, emerging from the darkness, is illuminated by the light from a burning building. But when he watches the repeat news later, he sees it is someone else, another girl.

Minnie Flynn, Sam says to himself. Minnie Flynn.

The Franklands do not sell the house, not yet anyway.

The weather looks set for another record-breaking summer: the flip side, as Dan says, of the greenhouse effect. In this benign sunshine it is hard to worry about the ozone layer. Kate worries, of course, in a semi-professional way, but at least that is better than worrying about what will happen to Sheila when Howard drops her.

In May Dan decides to fill the pool while they can, before the drought restrictions come in. He has had the cracked tiles repaired, he checks the filters and chemicals himself, and now there is a pool party of the kind they used to have long ago. Horseman has prescribed swimming but Dan's decision has

190

nothing to do with that. He knows he will always have back trouble from the fall after Lucy died, but it is a wound he will live with.

It is hardly a party: simply friends coming together to swim. The Summersons come plus Sheila, who goes topless and wears, below, a minimal scrap of cloth the size of a man's handkerchief. My God, Moira says to Kate, does she shave her pubic hair? Kate, who has put Sheila into a daughterly relationship, is not amused. Then she grins and confesses: she hasn't actually got any.

The Krafts are there too. And all the children. Around the pool in various attitudes. Talking, sipping wine, sunning, waiting for something, it seems to Moira. She looks round. Everyone is waiting for someone to take the plunge.

Kate is fitting Poppy's water-wings. Morris Kraft and Howard Summerson are trying to get the barbecue going. Sam is sprawled on his stomach on the grass talking to Sally. Donny is with them. As they talk he is pulling at the already balding lawn. Judith is stretched out on a lounger. The sun has greyed her chestnut hair and she has not bothered to tint it, but she is still beautiful. Well, Moira thinks, we are all older, and that is not entirely unwelcome.

Dan is standing a little apart at the far end of the pool in the shadow of the house. From here Moira cannot see his face but his posture is familiar: hands on hips, spine stretched for the good of his back. Barney, sensible dog, dozing close to Dan, in the shade.

The sky is blue but the pool reflects a sky that never was, bluer than any blue dreamed of by God.

'Dan,' Moira calls and he waves and takes a step to the edge of the deep end.

Moira raises her Polaroid and at the same moment Judith stands and reaches for the bottle of wine on the ground between the loungers.

'Oh, but we must do this properly!'

As Moira takes her picture, Judith makes her propitiatory libation to the pool and Dan dives.

So a minute or so after the event, Moira ejects the photograph. It shows Judith blinded by sun as she pours the wine,

191

the goddess of the pool, an arm raised above her eyes. And Dan caught a little out of focus in mid-dive between blue sky and bluer pool. There they are, frozen for ever, as if that were the last thing that happened, for as long as the print does not fade. So she will be able to take it out and think: that is how we were, once upon a time.